Mama stood staring at the watch, frowning. Suddenly we heard the sound of a twig snapping, as if being trod underfoot. Mama dropped the watch. "Shh!" she said, holding her finger to her lips. "Listen!" It came again, a sharp snap, then another, followed by a rustling in the brush ahead and to the left.

A deer, I thought. *It had to be a deer.* I touched Mama's arm. "It's a deer, and if we stand still it'll come out of the shadows so that we can see it." I reached out to Mama. Together we stood, frozen, waiting. After what seemed an eternity, we sensed something close by, watching.

There was a faint rustling again as a shadowy figure crept closer. For a moment we stared, barely able to discern the shape from the surrounding shadows. The figure stopped and my blood ran cold.

Other Holloway House Novels by Nora DeLoach:

Silas
Mama Solves A Murder

MAMA
TRAPS A
KILLER

Nora L. DeLoach

An Original Holloway House Edition
HOLLOWAY HOUSE PUBLISHING COMPANY
LOS ANGELES, CALIFORNIA

Published by
HOLLOWAY HOUSE PUBLISHING COMPANY
8060 Melrose Avenue, Los Angeles, California 90046

This is a work of fiction. Names, characters, places, and incidents
are either the product of the author's imagination or are used fic-
titiously. Any resemblance to actual events or locales or persons,
living or dead, is entirely coincidental.

International Standard Book Number 0-87067-747-0
Printed in the United States of America

Cover photograph by Jeffrey. Posed by professional model.
Cover design by Paul M. Papp.

To
The International Black Writers Association,
Atlanta, Georgia,
Edna Crutchfield, Founder,
and the kind editor and publisher that every author
dreams about but rarely finds.

MAMA TRAPS A KILLER

Prologue

June 19th. Evening shadows scattered through dancing silhouettes. Squirrels scrambled, rabbits listened, fawns and does moved gracefully among the pines. Danny Jones lay in tall grass and matted leaves. His clothes were torn; raccoons and small animals invaded his body. Scavenger birds flew low over his head; beetles feasted on his skin. Green flies, spiders, mites, and millipedes swarmed his face. Danny Jones did not move; he had a hole through his chest. His hair and nails were loose; his skin had burst open; in a few days, he would be skeletonized. A gentle breeze stirred. It blew through the forest, filling the June air with the odor of decomposed flesh.

Chapter One

It was early May. A silky sunrise had kissed the Atlanta morning sky, but by midday the weather had become overcast and gray. It was Friday, the first. I had finally completed drafting a brief for my boss to review over the weekend, dropped it off at the office to be typed, and swung onto Interstate 20. I turned the radio to KISS 104.7; it was exactly 12:20. I headed east toward Augusta, where I took highway 125 into Allendale. There I swung off onto highway 278 through Fairfax and Brunson before I ended up at my parents' home in Hampton. The temperature held steady at seventy-five degrees; the threat of rain never did become a downpour of hard wet water. The clouds and humidity just blanketed Georgia and South Carolina as if waiting until nightfall to bring the deluge.

I love driving into the low country of South Carolina. The farmers' neatly furrowed cornfields and trenches of small sprouts of watermelon confirmed the approach of summer. The reason for this trip was not to admire the farmers' handiwork. My mama had summoned me to help her prepare for my parents' first income-tax audit.

By five o'clock, Mama and I were sitting at the kitchen table, where she was neatly stacking dated medical bills. Her brow was uncommonly furrowed in a frown. "I don't know what they want from poor people," she grumbled.

My mother's name is Grace but everybody calls her "Candi" because of her complexion, a golden brown color with yellow undertones that looks as smooth as silk.

While Mama separated receipts, I sat looking out the window watching streaks of sun dart back and forth through clouds. It was time to plan for a vacation—fun in the sun, I thought.

My eyes wandered toward the basketball hoop my brothers had put up so that they could play ball whenever they came home. That was a seldom occasion, so for the most part Daddy's first cousin Eric used it. Today, Eric was playing with a boy I had never seen before. He looked almost eighteen, although he had a childlike face that didn't match his body. His movements were so awkward and uncoordinated that he stumbled and fell often, which seemed to annoy Eric.

Mama interrupted my thoughts. "Simone, I don't know why the IRS always bothers poor people."

"Because poor people are the ones who pay income taxes," I said. "Rich people know how to use loopholes."

"I can't find any more receipts," she said. "If these won't do, I just don't know…."

I nodded, remembering the huge medical bills my parents had incurred several years earlier when my father had surgery for bleeding ulcers. He had refused to go to Charleston to the VA hospital because he considered it minor surgery. The doctor had said he would be in and out of the hospital in a few days. In fact, however, Daddy almost died because he started bleeding internally, and that had to be stopped before surgery. The whole ordeal grew larger than expected, and it ended up costing my parents thousands of dollars, dollars that the IRS wanted verified.

"Mama," I said, changing the subject, "who is that boy?"

For a moment Mama stopped fiddling with the receipts and looked out the window. She gave a quick laugh. "He's not very good, is he?" she said.

"I can't believe a black boy would play basketball that badly," I said.

"His name is Danny Jones," she said, then turned back and began looking through receipts again.

"I don't remember seeing him around before," I said.

"He's been hanging around for a couple of weeks," she said, her voice low and deliberate. "He's here so often lately, you'd think he was one of the family."

"He reminds me of somebody," I said, shaking my head at seeing Eric elbow the boy in the stomach.

Mama looked up. "James says he reminds him of your brothers," she said.

"I don't know about that," I said, looking closer. "He sure doesn't play ball like my brothers!"

"He doesn't play ball like anybody I've ever seen," she said somewhat sarcastically.

"Where is he from?" I asked, wondering how could my father think that my brothers ever looked that awkward.

"Ridgeland," she said, knocking a neat stack of receipts to the floor. "For god sake, Simone," she snapped, "come away from that window and help me get these doctor bills together!"

My name is Simone Covington. I'm the youngest of my parents' three children, their only daughter. My brothers don't get pulled into Mama's adventures like I do. It's because Mama and I have this thing, a sense of seeing beyond the obvious. Sometimes I find our talent fascinating, sometimes troublesome, but most times I have to yield to it.

Most of the things that arouse the mind don't excite me or Mama but we do become euphoric when our minds are deducing. We're self-styled private investigators who enjoy the tedious job of digging up bits and pieces of information until we've solved a puzzle. Long ago, I don't remember when, Mama convinced me that, if we could get at the truth of a problem, we would make a contribution to society.

I started writing our adventures last year when we solved murders in South Carolina and Atlanta. At that time, I told how the sheriff in Hampton County had

13

fallen under Mama's spell a few months after Daddy moved her to town. It happened when Mama was driving on that long stretch of road, highway 601, that leads into Hampton from Estill and Nixville. Mama got a flat tire just before Sheriff Abe drove by. He stopped to help and Mama hit him with a double barrel of sweetness, following it up with the delivery of a sweet potato pie. One pie led to another until Mama became a frequent visitor to his office. Between sweet potato pies and conversations, Mama helped the sheriff solve several crimes, so he grew to respect her intuition as much as he liked her cooking.

Eight weeks after I watched the awkward Danny Jones play ball with Eric in my parents' backyard, I had to go back for another visit. It was June nineteenth. My parents' first trip to the IRS had been unsatisfactory; they hadn't been able to produce enough receipts to justify their deduction. They were given a second appointment with the mandate to come up with more receipts or pay back taxes and a penalty. Mama was infuriated and, when she called me back home, I thought it was to prime her on the tax laws. You see, I'm a paralegal and, while I work for a defense lawyer and tax laws aren't my forte, I have the means to find out just how far the IRS could push.

When I arrived home late Friday night, I wasn't prepared for what Mama had on her mind; it was not income taxes.

"Do you really want to do this?" I asked, watching Mama vigorously knead bread dough. "I came home to help you get ready for your appointment with the

IRS, not to go with you tomorrow morning to the state hospital to visit a woman who has lost her mind!"

"She has had a nervous breakdown, Simone," she said, moving the bread back and forth with her fist, "and if we go first thing in the morning, we'll be back in time for you to get back to Atlanta early afternoon. You can spend all day Sunday with Cliff!"

"One of the women in town has had a nervous breakdown, and you feel obligated to visit her at the state hospital?"

Mama ignored my tone. One by one, she placed perfectly round yeast rolls onto the baking pan. "We've got to visit her," she said. She put the rolls onto the counter and covered them with cheesecloth; time was needed for them to rise. She washed her hands and I thought of her as a high priestess among the implements of her craft. There was no consulting cook books, just a brief laying of her hands on each ingredient like a blessing.

I sat, my hands cradling my second cup of coffee.

"Simone, you okay?" she asked.

I shook my head. "If I had known that you wanted me to go with you to the state hospital, I wouldn't have come home this weekend."

Mama turned. "That's why I didn't tell you before you made the trip."

"Don't you think this visit is taking a neighborly gesture a little too far?" I asked.

"Lucy is not just a neighbor," she said. "She's Danny's aunt!"

"Danny who?"

"Danny Jones, you remember," she said.

I shook my head.

"The boy from Ridgeland," she said. "You saw him playing basketball with Eric a couple of months ago…, the tall clumsy boy!"

I nodded. "Okay, okay," I said, finally remembering. "But, I still can't see why you've got to visit his aunt in the mental hospital."

"Because he's been missing since June sixth or seventh," she said. "Everybody in town is worried about the boy."

"An aunt in the state hospital would be the last person I would expect to know where Danny has been for two weeks."

"Maybe she can help me, maybe she can't," Mama said.

"What connection does she have with Danny other than being his aunt?" I asked.

"Both Danny and his mother, Esther, lived with Lucy," she answered. "A few days after Danny's disappearance, Lucy had her nervous breakdown. Most of the time she says things that don't make any sense, but one thing that she keeps repeating is that something terrible has happened to Danny."

"What does Danny's mother say about his absence?"

"Nothing much."

"She probably thinks that she'll hear from him eventually, like she probably will."

"Miss Carrie…," Mama started to say.

I interrupted and pointed toward the house across

the street. "You mean that nosy old woman that lives over there?"

Mama nodded. "Miss Carrie told me that Lucy and Esther lived in Camp Branch most of their lives. When their parents died nobody in the family would take the girls except their aunt and uncle. Lucy has always been nervous but Esther seemed pretty strong. The aunt and uncle got so old that they couldn't take care of themselves, so Esther assumed responsibility for the family. One summer, according to Miss Carrie, the two old people died within two weeks of each other. Almost nine months to the day, Esther delivered a boy, Danny. Nobody knows who Danny's father is," Mama said, her voice dropping.

"Probably some married man," I said.

Mama sighed. "Anyway, when Danny started school Esther moved to Ridgeland, where she took care of some old white people. About three months ago, the people died and she couldn't find work, so she moved back in the house with Lucy."

"Maybe Danny didn't like it in Camp Branch and decided to go back to Ridgeland," I said.

"I wish that was true," Mama said.

The apprehension in Mama's tone startled me. "What do you mean?" I said.

"Danny's been hanging around here ever since he's moved back from Ridgeland," she said.

"So, he likes your cooking."

"It's not my cooking," she said, leaning forward in her chair. "It's James!"

"Daddy?"

Mama cleared her throat. "Yes," she said. "For some reason, Danny took a liking to James and, at least two or three times a week, he would come and sit outside in our front yard waiting for James to get home from work. When James arrived, they would sit in his car for hours. Sometimes they talked so long that James' supper got cold."

"And Daddy has never invited the boy into the house?"

"He says he has," she said. "It's one of the things that annoys me about Danny. You know I don't like people sitting out in cars in front of the house. I tried to get James to bring the boy inside, but he said the boy refused to come in."

I hesitated, remembering that my father had left the day before for his annual trip to reserve camp. "It doesn't sound like my father to be spending that much time with a boy that age."

"That's not the worst of it," Mama continued. "James has given him money, I know it."

"Did you ask Daddy about that?"

"Of course I did, but James just said that I'm making too much over nothing. He claims that all these years I've been helping people and, now that he's decided to help Danny, I'm finding fault."

"What do you think?"

Mama shook her head. "I don't know," she said, a strange look in her eyes. "I think there's more to it than James admits, if that's what you mean." She sighed. "James never treated our boys like he does Danny. He was always too busy or away...."

I waited, then asked, "It bothers you that the boys are not close to you or Daddy, doesn't it?"

Mama ignored my question and seemed to regain her composure. "There's one thing for sure," she said, "I must agree with James that, if Danny had simply moved away, he would have told him!"

I didn't like the way Mama's words sounded nor the way they were making me feel.

"What do you mean?" I asked.

"James swears the boy had no intention of leaving Camp Branch," she said. "He says that he got Danny a job with Jimmy Holstein at the Ford place but Danny never showed up."

"I suppose you've already talked to Jimmy Holstein?"

She nodded. "He confirms that he interviewed and hired Danny. He expected the boy to show up for work June eighth."

"Based on Daddy's and Lucy's allegations, you think that something has happened to the boy."

"It's worth looking into, since both James and Lucy obstinately insist that there is more to Danny's missing than leaving home to see the world."

I took a deep breath, then waved my hands in submission. "All right," I said. "You've convinced me that we might need to look into Danny's disappearance, but why do we have to visit his aunt?"

Mama's head dropped. She seemed tense, but the impression was so fleeting that I almost felt I had imagined it. "Because James asked me to talk to her," she said quietly.

"*Daddy* asked you?"

"He said that Lucy might be able to tell me something that could help us find Danny."

"That's a twist," I said. "He *wants* us to sleuth?"

"I guess," she said.

"Just why is your husband so concerned about Danny Jones?" I asked. "It's hard for me to believe that he got that close to the boy in just a few months!"

Mama hesitated just a fraction of a second. "He's gotten close enough to offer a five-thousand-dollar reward if anybody finds the boy alive," she said.

I whistled. "You're kidding, aren't you?" I said. "My father, the county's biggest tightwad, is willing to pay five thousand dollars to find a boy that is no kin to him.... I don't believe it!"

Mama frowned. For a moment neither of us spoke. Finally she shrugged. "I don't care what you say, James is right. If something has happened to Danny, it's our duty to discover what it is!"

"What you mean," I said, "is that you want to know why Daddy is so interested in Danny's whereabouts, isn't it?"

"I don't know which is worse on me, James' insistence that I find Danny or the IRS' insistence that we've lied about a few medical deductions."

"Don't worry about the IRS," I said, waving my hand away from Mama. "The worst thing that can happen with that is that you and Daddy could go to jail." I laughed; Mama grimaced.

"That's not funny," she said.

"You can go to Young's drugstore and ask for

receipts of all your drug purchases if he's kept them that far back. And you can ask Dr. Sanford to give you a running account of what you paid him over the past couple of years."

"I'll do that the first thing Monday morning," she said.

"Mama," I asked, changing the subject, "didn't you tell me that nobody knows the identity of Danny's father?"

"That's right," she said.

"I wonder…?" I said, trying to think of who might be the mysterious man who had visited Esther over eighteen years before and left her pregnant with a son…, a son that my father was now extremely concerned about.

Chapter Two

When I awoke the next morning I lay still, the thoughts of the previous night swirling in my head. I enjoy waking up in Hampton, being away from the rumbling noises of rush-hour traffic. Today, the cool dawn's air and the sounds of daybreak did little to clear my head. I got out of bed, slipped into my robe, and left my room to go to the kitchen.

The clock on the wall showed five-thirty. I moved as quietly as possible, glancing now and then through the window at the sky. I wanted to get out while the morning was still dark. By six o'clock I was sitting on the front porch sipping a hot cup of coffee watching the break of day as it kissed the horizon.

I had an ominous feeling, like I was losing something valuable.

An hour later, I walked into the house. Mama was at the stove cooking what she considered a light breakfast: coffee, orange juice, toast, and eggs.

"Are you sure we need to be going to Columbia today?" I asked. "I don't feel good about it."

Mama stopped working at the stove and turned to face me. She said nothing but made a tiny movement of the head that I took to mean we were going to Columbia anyway.

"The trip may be useless," I said, going over and picking up the coffee pot and refilling my mug with coffee. "Lucy may be so disoriented that she doesn't even remember Danny."

There was a rare look on Mama's face. "James asked me to talk to her and I promised him that I would do it."

I took the mug over to the table and sat. "It's bothering you that Daddy is so interested in Danny, isn't it? You think it's strange that he's offering a five-thousand-dollar reward to find a boy who's only been around a couple of months."

Mama flinched; her brow rose. She poured herself a mug of coffee, then joined me at the table. "*Alive*," she said with emphasis. "James made it clear that he'll pay the five thousand dollars if Danny is found alive."

"So, if Danny's dead, Daddy is no longer interested in the boy?"

Mama's expression darkened. "Do you know how that sounds?"

"Daddy could know that the boy is dead and that he'll never have to shell out all that money."

23

Mama flinched. "You sound like you're accusing your father of doing something to Danny."

"I don't believe it doesn't bother you that Daddy is willing to spend that much money to find this boy!"

Mama looked undaunted. "It's not like James to become that involved with people, but his motives are good."

"He's always scolded us for being good Samaritans. It's hard to believe he's treating this young man better than he treated his sons!"

"James was good to all three of his children."

"He was good to me, but to the boys...."

Mama interrupted. "He wanted his boys to become soldiers, like he was!" She paused. "You're trying to get me away from wanting to go see Lucy, but it won't work, young lady. We're going to Columbia and that's that!"

An hour and a half later, we were driving down highway 278 to Fairfax, where we took a right turn on 321 straight into Columbia. It was eleven o'clock when we pulled up into the parking lot of the state hospital.

The main entrance to the hospital was a single glass door. Stepping inside, we found ourselves in the lobby. To our right was a small window with a large woman sitting behind a desk.

"What do you want?" she asked as we approached.

Mama pulled out an official looking piece of paper she had gotten from Sheriff Abe and handed it to the woman. She read it, then told us to wait. A few minutes later, she came out with a husky woman who was dressed in hospital greens. The woman had a strong jaw and cold gray, threatening eyes.

Mama smiled as we were introduced. "Follow me," the woman said, her voice as husky as her body. She motioned us toward the door at the far end of the room, which led us into a corridor with glaring lights so bright that it took a few minutes for our eyes to adjust. Several women were mopping a tan tiled floor. "Watch your step," our guide ordered. The walls were tan-painted cinder blocks. The smell of disinfectant filled the air.

After what seemed like a long walk, we turned down another bright corridor. One side of the wall was solid concrete, the other side was lined with small rooms that looked like tiny cells. Each room had one occupant. Some knelt, some stood, others lay in the fetal position. All moaned, giggled, or made some kind of sound.

The attendant stopped us at a room at the end of the hall. "This is Lucy Jones," she said, taking a key from her pocket and opening the door. "I'll be standing up there," she pointed to the other end of the corridor. "If you need me, just holler."

There were two straight-back chairs in Lucy's room and a cot that was her bed. I was surprised that there were chairs in Lucy's room. There was no linen, just a flat, bare mattress. Lucy sat on the edge of the cot, a drugged look in her eyes. She looked like a tiny rag doll, with her bare legs and flat shoes. She clutched her elbows close to her body.

25

A lump welled up in my throat. I stared at Mama and wondered what she could expect to learn from this poor woman.

Mama spoke in a low but strong voice. "Lucy," she said, "we're looking for Danny."

Lucy began breathing heavily. "Something bad has happened to him," she said, looking down at her hands.

"What do you think has happened?" she asked.

"He used to go out in the woods," Lucy said.

"Is that where he is now?" Mama asked, watching Lucy's reaction.

"In the middle of the night," Lucy whispered, "in the woods in the middle of the night."

"Which woods?" Mama asked.

Lucy changed; her voice became childlike. "He ain't gone no place," she said. "He's home safe with his mama. Tell his mama that he ain't gone no place!"

"What do you mean?" Mama asked.

Lucy's eyes skated between Mama and me. Her voice turned cold. "It's that look!"

"What look?"

Lucy began biting her lower lip. "Something bad has happened to Danny," she said. "He ain't gone!"

At that moment, the woman in the next room screamed, which set off a commotion of screaming voices all along the corridor. The attendant who had led us in shouted, "Shut up!" and the chants stopped. The low moans and giggles began again.

Mama leaned in her chair, her eyes riveted onto Lucy's face. "What makes you think something bad has happened to Danny?" she asked.

"Lucy's eyes twitched; she turned her head to a dubious angle, which made it look like she was suppressing a smile. "Something bad has happened to Danny," she whispered, then threw her head back and let out a laugh that echoed throughout the corridors.

"Maybe Danny has found his father," Mama said when Lucy stopped laughing.

Lucy looked down at her hands; her chin quivered.

"His father," Mama repeated. "Maybe Danny has gone to visit his father."

The lump in my throat grew larger. Mama's voice was soft and gentle, but I could tell she wanted Lucy to say something about Danny's father. "I want to find Danny," she said. "Maybe his father can tell me where he is."

"He ain't gone," Lucy snapped.

"Lucy, I need your help."

"No!" Lucy screamed, "He ain't gone…." Her voice trailed off. Her body became rigid, but her eyes moved.

The husky attendant walked up to the door and looked at her watch. I swallowed. "We'd better go," I suggested.

Mama nodded and stood up. For a moment she hesitated, then walked to the door. I followed. The attendant opened the door and, after relocking it, she led us through the corridors toward the front entrance.

A half hour later, we were driving to Hampton. Mama stared out of the window into the sky. I wanted to talk. "What do you think about what Lucy said?" I asked. I waited for Mama to answer, but she remained silent. I waited for a few minutes, then tried again. "What do you think about our visit with Lucy?" I repeated, this time a little louder.

"What?" Mama said distractedly.

"Lucy's visit..., what do you think?"

"I don't," she said. "She said some strange things, didn't she?"

"Why did you ask her about Danny's father?" I asked.

"I don't know," she said.

"You think Danny is Daddy's son, don't you?"

There was a wondering expression on her face. "I have to be honest with you, Simone," she said. "It's possible."

"You're kidding!"

"James was stationed in Fort Dix the year before Danny's birth. He visited Hampton twice, staying two weeks once and three weeks the other time. I remember not joining him on either trip, once because you were sick and the other time because I couldn't get off from work."

"So, it's possible that he is...."

"It's possible, but I don't believe it."

"You've asked Daddy?"

"Yes," she said.

"And?"

She took a deep breath. "He denies having an affair with Esther."

"Could he be lying?"

"James is not a liar, Simone."

"Well, maybe not lying, but...."

"He's holding something back, I'm sure, if that's what you mean."

"I never imagined my father with another woman...."

Mama interrupted again. "Simone, your father is a good husband."

"I always wanted a husband like my father."

"You'll get a good one if he's like James," she said.

The next time Mama said anything to me we were driving up into her driveway. "I guess you'll be going to Atlanta now," she said.

"You sound anxious for me to leave."

She smiled.

"I'll get my overnight bag and hit the road," I said, winking. "If I hurry, I'll get home in time for Cliff and me to plan something special for our Sunday together."

"How's Sidney?" she asked as she followed me into the house. My boss and my mother had become good friends.

"He's okay," I said. Mama walked toward the kitchen while I headed for my bedroom, a bedroom that Mama had kept as I had left it when I went off to college.

I stood in the middle of the room and felt the security of my family threatened. *Danny Jones is Daddy's son*, I thought. *My brother.*

I shook my head and sighed, then walked down the hall to the front door. Mama must have heard me, because she came out of the kitchen and met me.

"I expect James to be calling soon," she said, looking beyond my forehead. "I'll just tell him that you had to leave early."

For a moment, it seemed that we both felt awkward. Then Mama reached for me and pulled me close to her body. We hugged and, for the first time in my life, I felt my mother's body tremble. "It's going to be all right," she whispered. "We're going to get to the bottom of this thing and our family will be all right again."

The phone rang. "It's James now," she said, moving away from me and toward the kitchen. I followed. She picked up the receiver and listened, said okay, then put the phone onto the hook. "It was Abe," she said, her voice apprehensive. "A hunter found Danny's body in the woods an hour ago!"

Chapter Three

A few minutes later, we were driving south on highway 278 to 68 out of Varnville toward Camp Branch. After we passed Varnville, we drove another five or six miles until we reached a crossroads, where we made a right onto a dirt road cut through by loggers. We drove almost two miles farther. I stared through the window at the woods until I could see the sheriff's patrol car.

We stepped out of the car and walked toward the middle of a huge circle of pine trees. Danny Jones' torn body lay where it had been found. One of the sheriff's deputies was taking pictures; another was using a stick to poke around in the underbrush.

Sheriff Abe stood in the middle of the clearing shaking his head. Mama walked over and laid a reassuring hand on his shoulder. "I've never seen anything like that before," he said. "I've looked at a lot of bodies, but this one is in the worst condition I've ever seen."

A smothering heat blanketed the air with the smell of death. Squirrels sprinted back and forth, birds squawked, flies and yellow jackets swarmed the body, and all I could think about was the tall, awkward boy playing basketball in my parents' backyard. I walked to the car; I felt like I was going to vomit.

After a few minutes, Mama walked toward the car. "Abe said that they've found a red bandanna and some kind of wooden whistle," she said.

"Clues?"

"They belonged to Danny," she said, frowning slightly.

"What's the matter?" I asked, responding to her expression.

"I'm not sure," she said, her expression clearing. "There's something about this whole thing that doesn't set right with me!"

For a moment neither of us spoke.

"Can we go now?" I asked.

"Abe wants me to visit Danny's mother, Esther," she said. "He said I might do a better job of telling her that his body had been found than he or one of his deputies."

I nodded, anxious to get out of there. "Let's go now," I said.

We got in the car, pulled onto the road, and turned the car around. Though these woods were in the back of Danny's house, the house was approachable from an adjacent highway.

When we drove up into the Joneses' yard, there was a strange silence. For one thing, the chicken coop was without chickens and the hog pen had no pigs. Hardened clay was swept clean all around the house up to the edge of the woods. Farther back, I could see a fragment of what looked like a chimney. Beyond the chimney, there was a forest of thick growth and pine trees. You could neither see nor hear the sheriff or his deputies. If I had not seen it with my eyes, I wouldn't have known that Danny Jones' body lay in the woods behind his house.

In the July heat, I found myself shivering just thinking about Danny. As if she had read my mind, Mama reached over and patted me on the shoulder.

Esther Jones opened the front door before we knocked, a knowing look on her face. She waved us inside and shut the door. The house was cool. Inside the front door was a large room with faded blue wallpaper. In contrast, there were new curtains hanging at the window facing the front of the house.

Esther Jones was a woman of about fifty; the upper portion of her hair was dyed black, but new growth of gray pushed out around her head so that the black hair looked liked a top hat. She wore a shapeless dress that hung loosely on her body. She looked strong and muscular.

Esther sat down in a rocking chair next to the window and began rocking. I cleared my throat and sat in a straight-back chair next to a large wooden table.

Mama walked over to Esther and knelt by the chair. "They found Danny," she whispered to Esther.

Esther pulled away and groaned. "Where?" she asked.

"In the woods, on the other side, behind the house," Mama said.

Esther looked at Mama halfway with her eyes; her mind was someplace else.

Mama nodded. "I'm so sorry," she said. "Sheriff Abe asked me to tell you."

Esther looked like she wanted to speak but forgot how to. For a moment she seemed to be concentrating on getting the words out. Then her eyes widened, her lips twisted, and she spoke. "Crazy Joe," she said.

Mama stood up and gave Esther a suspicious look. "Who is Crazy Joe?" she asked.

Esther's lips moved but there was no sound. She sat rocking back and forth, staring out of the window, and I could tell that she was not going to say any more.

"Does Crazy Joe live around here?" Mama asked.

Esther didn't respond. Her body stiffened; again she opened her mouth but still no words came out. Her lips twitched. I could see the muscles in her throat tighten. *She's going to pass out*, I thought.

At that moment, there was a knock on the front door. I swallowed.

"Who is it?" Mama asked.

"Rose."

"I'll get it," I said. A blast of hot air pushed through the room as a big woman walked in the front door. Rose, we soon learned, was Esther's closest neighbor.

Rose's complexion was the color of rutabagas, her hair hung over her shoulders, her eyes were an eerie gray, and her wide mouth was accentuated with bright red lipstick.

Esther sat staring at Rose while tears streamed down her face. Rose's eyes shifted from Esther to Mama and to Esther again. "Esther," she asked, "are you all right?"

Esther stared in bewilderment; obviously she wasn't sure of the answer.

"Esther," Rose said, forcing a smile, "everything is going to be all right."

Esther began crying; she shook her head, her lips quivered, her hands shook. "Danny's dead," she blurted out, wiping her cheeks.

Rose reached down and began rubbing Esther's shoulders. "He was a good boy," she said. "Danny was a good boy and everybody knew it."

Esther stared down in her lap. "What am I going to do without my Danny?" she asked, her voice quivering. "What am I going to do without my boy?"

"The Lord will help you," Rose said.

"I want him back," Esther wailed. She looked out of the window. "I want Danny to come home right now. He's been out in those woods too long. It'll soon be night; he should be home by now. Why won't he listen to me anymore? Danny knows not to stay out in those woods too long...."

"Where are your pills?" Rose asked, looking around the room. "Dr. Tuten gave her pills for her nerves when Lucy...."

"I'll get water," I said, moving toward the kitchen. I stood looking out of the window, running a glass of water, when I noticed something in the woods directly in my line of vision, something that looked like a green car parked deep inside a circle of trees. At first it looked like a shadow, tight between the trees. I put the glass down and stared through the window, trying to make sure of what I was seeing. It was a late model, and at first I wondered what it was doing back there. I shrugged and finished filling the glass. Maybe that's how people bury their old cars, I thought.

By the time I returned to the room with the water, Rose had found the pills. She stood over Esther, with pills in hands. I handed her the glass. She made Esther take the pills and drink all the water.

Frightened, Esther looked into Rose's face. After a few moments, she spoke. "Please make Danny come home from the woods," she said. "It's getting late and he ain't got no business out there at night."

"He'll be all right," Rose said, pulling Esther from the chair. "Now come on into the bedroom and lie down," she said. Mama reached for Esther's other arm, but Esther pulled away. Mama smiled, but Esther looked into Rose's face.

"Tell Danny to come home," she whispered.

"After you rest," Rose said. "After you take a rest." Rose led Esther into the bedroom, where they stayed for almost fifteen minutes. After a while, Rose came out of the room.

"She's asleep," she said. "One of those pills knocks you out for hours; two will knock you out for days.

36

The poor woman. She's had her share of tragedy!"

Mama nodded.

"Don't worry," Rose said. "We'll take care of her. Now that Danny's gone and Lucy's in the crazy house, well it's a wonder...."

Mama interrupted. "Who is Crazy Joe?" Mama asked.

Rose laughed. "He's old man People's grandson; he's harmless. Why?"

"Esther mentioned that he might be responsible for Danny's death," she said.

Rose shook her head. "I doubt it," she said. "He was in the war and came home shell-shocked, but that was almost twenty years ago. He talks to himself a little, hangs around the edge of the woods, but he ain't bothered nobody before."

"You don't think he killed Danny?" Mama asked.

"I can't believe it," Rose said, her voice a bit too protective. "If he'd wanted to kill anybody, he'd done it long before now. Anyway, he liked Danny."

"You've seen him with Danny?"

Rose started to shake her head, then changed her mind. "Yeah," she began. "I've seen them together plenty of times. Danny was the only person who could get close to Crazy Joe, and he liked the boy. Danny once told me that Crazy Joe had shown him every nook and cranny of these woods." She shook her head. "I'd be hard pressed to think that Crazy Joe would hurt the boy."

Mama's brow knitted into a thoughtful frown. "Who then?" Mama asked.

Rose stood thinking. "I don't know," she admitted. "We're a small community here; everybody knows everybody all their lives. I can't imagine why anybody would want to hurt the boy."

"Maybe a stranger," I said.

"Could be," Rose said. "These days and times strange people are most everywhere, but I think it was a hunter, a freak accident."

"What do you mean?" I asked.

Rose's brows had risen a notch. "You know, somebody hunting and mistaking the boy for a deer. It happened in Scotia a few weeks ago. Man shot and killed his best friend, thinking he was a deer."

"That sounds possible," I whispered, looking into Mama's eyes. She stood, looking and considering. "We visited Lucy today," Mama said when she spoke, "and she seemed to have known that Danny had died in the woods."

"What did she say?" Rose asked.

"It arouses suspicion in my mind," she said.

Rose shook her head. "Danny's death doesn't make any sense if it wasn't an accident," Rose said.

"If we believe Lucy," Mama said, "it wasn't an accident."

Rose raised her brow and forced a weak smile. "Lucy's a bit strange," Rose said. "Always has been. I remember when the old people died...."

"Who?"

"The Joneses, the people who raised Lucy and Esther."

"What happened?"

"Lucy carried on the same way she is now, and Esther ended up having to put her away then too."

Mama paused, considering. "I didn't know that," she said, her voice quiet.

"Stayed in Columbia for almost a year after they died," Rose said. "It was after Danny was born that the poor woman came to her senses."

My heart raced. I took a deep breath, trying to control my emotions. "So that's why she doesn't know who Danny's father is?" I asked.

Rose's voice dropped to a whisper. "Nobody knows," she said. "I was staying in New York at the time, but I talked to Miss Audrey, the midwife who delivered the boy, and she said that nobody ever seen a man come or go from Esther's place."

"Esther never told you who Danny's father was?" I asked, my heart still pounding.

Rose rolled her eyes. "Esther never told anybody who the boy's father was. Oh, she bragged about him enough though. Used to say that he was somebody important, that he had plenty of money, and that he was some kind of big shot. But nobody around here ever seen a man visit her, big or little shot." She chuckled.

I took a deep breath. "So you can't think of anybody particular around that time who might have gotten Esther pregnant?" I asked.

"No," Rose said, holding on to the word a bit longer than I expected.

Mama looked at her watch. "I guess we'd better be going," she said.

Rose nodded.

"If Esther needs anything…" Mama said.

"Don't worry about her," Rose said, patting Mama on her shoulder. "Esther is like family to me…. I'll take care of her."

She walked us to the front porch and waved good-bye as we drove off.

Chapter Four

Even though I drove to Atlanta Saturday night, I didn't call my boyfriend, Cliff. I spent the entire Sunday moping around my apartment, trying not to believe that my father would offer a reward for Danny knowing that the boy had been dead and that nobody would claim the reward.

Monday morning I woke up with my eyes blinking at the gray streaks of light shining through the blinds of my bedroom. For a long moment, I resisted awakening at all, for as consciousness returned, so did the gnawing feeling that my father had something to do with Danny Jones' death.

The morning was rainy, the droppings from heavy clouds tapping a mournful dirge on the apartment's roof.

For a long time I didn't want to move at all, but I knew I had to give up the wish to shrink into the warm escape of sleep. I stirred, then eased myself up and went to the window to look out into the gray Atlanta morning. Rain must have been falling all night because the streets were gullies filled with water.

By nine o'clock, I was running from my apartment to my Honda. The rain was streaking against the car and heavy clouds dimmed the daylight so that it almost looked like evening. I climbed into my car, put it in gear, turned on the windshield wipers, and eased out of the apartment complex onto South Hairston Parkway. I headed toward 285, barely seeing the pavement ahead.

It was the kind of day that fostered my sense of impending disaster—the vague feeling of panic I'd had since this business with Danny Jones had started. This morning I tried to ignore the feeling, but suddenly I felt the car lose its traction as I started into a corner. I stepped on the brake, then remembered it was the worst thing I could do and just as quickly released the pressure of my foot and steered into the skid. An eternal second later the tires caught again and I slowed to a crawl. I reached over and adjusted the rearview mirror so that I could look at my face. I took a deep breath, letting it out slowly, and wiped at my cheeks. The car keys jingled in the ignition. A few seconds later, I switched on the ignition again and drove off, determined to concentrate on driving.

By the time I arrived at the office, the rain had slowed to a drizzle and I had begun to relax a little.

My mind was longing to be in my apartment curled up with a book; it was one of the ways that I could forget things that troubled me.

I walked into my office, took my coat off, and hung it to dry. My next move was to switch on my computer. A note from my boss cut through my brooding thoughts. It was pinned next to the monitor, a familiar tacking place. I pushed past Sidney's secretary's desk and headed for the office lounge. I hadn't yet had my second cup of coffee.

Half an hour later, I walked into Sidney Jacoby's office. My boss was leaning back in his chair rubbing his chin. "I've got something for you to begin working on right away," he said. As he spoke, tiny flakes fell from his head onto his shoulders. He pushed a manila folder in front of me. Sidney Jacoby is a handsome white man, about fifty. He has dark brown eyes that can turn warm or cold, whichever he wants. His teeth gleam; he visits his dentist often to have them whitened. He wears his thick curly hair tapered at the neck and he has his fingernails manicured every week. The one flaw in his appearance is his dandruff, the constant fall of white flakes on his shoulders. Everybody who knows him well enough feels obliged to flick the dandruff from his jacket but, for some reason, the little white flakes don't bother Sidney himself.

I sat in the chair on the other side of Sidney's desk. "I'm all ears," I said, flipping through the manila folder.

Sidney frowned as if he sensed something nervous in me. His eyes seemed to narrow a little, then he glanced toward the wall of arranged books.

"You're frowning," I said. "Is the case you're about to brief me on that bad?"

Sidney turned his head to look at me, dandruff showering his Giorgio Armani navy blue suit. "It's a challenge," he said, "but you can meet it. We've got a new client, Thomas Matthews. He shot and killed Steven Foster a couple of weeks ago."

"Why?"

"Steven Foster tried to break into Thomas Matthews' house around three A.M. and, before he had a chance to complete his mission, Thomas Matthews shot and killed him."

I gave him a little wave of my hand. "Steven Foster shouldn't have been breaking into Thomas Matthews' house," I said.

A frustrated expression crept on Sidney's face. "The state attorney doesn't think that's a good enough reason to shoot and kill another person."

"The state attorney's office pressed charges?"

Sidney nodded, his face calm, expressionless.

"Foster had a gun?" I asked.

"The police didn't find one, but Matthews swears that Foster had a gun in his hand."

"Did Thomas Matthews know Steven Foster before the attempted break-in?"

Sidney shook his head. "Says the first time he laid eyes on Foster was that evening."

"Are there witnesses?"

"One. Thomas Matthews' wife."

"What does she say?"

"The same thing as her husband."

"You want to know everything about Steven Foster," I said.

"From his birth."

"What about Thomas Matthews?"

"Do a routine background check but concentrate on Foster."

I lifted my hands in the air, palms up. "The whole world is crazy," I said, my voice more serious than I had intended.

Startled, Sidney looked up, his eyebrow arched. "What's eating you?" he asked.

I was looking toward the window but, out of the corner of my eye, I could see a skeptical look on Sidney's face, which told me that he was not going to be satisfied with my response.

"What's the matter with you?" he repeated.

I glanced up, surprised at the forcefulness of his tone. I took a deep, helpless breath and said, "Mama and I have a murder."

Sidney cocked his head in a familiar way, his eyes opened wide, his eyebrow raised. "Tell me about it," he said, taking a pencil from his drawer and reaching for a notepad.

I sighed. "It was a local boy," I said.

"Somebody close to your family?" he asked, writing down my words.

I cleared my throat. "He was close to my father," I said.

Sidney leaned in his chair and for a long moment looked me straight in the face. "A relative?"

"No. He just, I guess, took a liking to my father

and, well, he turned up in the woods behind his house. He had been shot."

Sidney frowned, then relaxed. "How long had he been dead?"

"About two weeks."

"In this heat, there can't be much left of him."

I shook my head and, when I spoke, the words surged like a torrent. "I saw Danny's body Saturday," I said, feeling my body shiver. "His eyes had been eaten out by birds, his flesh had been chewed away. It was the worst thing I've ever seen." I took a deep breath and tried to calm myself down. "Whoever killed the boy and left him in the woods like that should be...."

Sidney stopped writing and peered at me with a look of genuine concern. Shaking his head, his spoke in a low voice. "I'm sorry you had to see that," he said.

"I'll never forget the sight of that poor kid," I said, feeling myself shudder again.

Sidney stared at me in silence as if he was trying to think of something to say that would make my experience a little less depressing. "Does Candi have any ideas about the murder?" he asked.

I felt a wave of emotion, a deep compassion for my mother. "No," I admitted, feeling my body sink in my chair. "And this is such a bad time for her too."

"Why?"

I took a deep breath and leaned forward. "My parents are being audited by the Internal Revenue. It's their first time, and it's almost as traumatic for Mama as Danny's death has been."

"Do you think my accountant can help?"

I shook my head. "After their first meeting with IRS auditors, it all boils down to receipts for expensive medication that my father had to take when he had ulcer surgery a couple of years ago. I remember thinking how foolish he was not to go to the army hospital. He went to a private one, and they had to pay twenty percent of the hospital bills and all outpatient medication expenses. Mama keeps all her receipts but, for some reason, she can't find all of them. In fact, she can't even find her canceled checks to show that she paid for the medication."

"The pharmacist...."

I interrupted. "I've already suggested that she go to the local pharmacist and get him to give up receipts. I keep thinking that, with his receipts and maybe an affidavit, the IRS will be satisfied."

"Will she still have to pay?"

"Yeah, but not too much," I said. "It's just that the stress of the audit and now this...."

"Back to the death of the boy," Sidney said, stroking his chin. "Could it be somebody close to the boy, somebody in the family?"

"I doubt it," I said. "Danny doesn't have a family of that sort. He does have an aunt. We visited her in Columbia on Saturday."

Sidney's eyes widened.

"She's on Bull Street..., in the mental institution. So, besides seeing Danny's body, I visited his deranged aunt." I shook my head. "This was not a good weekend for me."

"Who is the other relative?" he asked.

"Danny's mother. She is a country woman, and she had nothing to gain and everything to lose by the death of her child." I frowned. "By the way, Mama and I had to break the news to her that Danny was dead."

"There is no father?" he asked, trying not to encourage my self-pity.

My shoulders slumped and I stirred in my seat. I made a pretense of considering the question, then shook my head.

"Then it's time to fan out," Sidney said. "Start looking at others close to the boy, perhaps a neighbor."

"His mother mentioned a Vietnam veteran named Crazy Joe, but the closest neighbor to the family doubts that he could be the culprit."

"Sounds like Candi has her hands full."

"More than you know," I whispered to myself.

"What?" Sidney asked.

"We'll get to the bottom of this thing," I said with a lot more confidence than I was feeling. Neither of us spoke for a full minute after that.

"You'll be needing to spend time with Candi?" he asked.

I nodded.

He swerved around in his overstuffed chair and looked out the window. Even though the rain had slowed, the blackness of the clouds made me shiver. "Work on the Matthews case," he said. "Be sure to check on the Roebling's pleading and…." He paused.

I grunted.

He turned and faced me, made a noncommittal gesture with his hands, and said, "Keep me informed of this murder case of yours!"

I nodded, grateful that I had a supportive boss. I stood up, my mind settling on the possibility of my father's indiscretion. "I appreciate your concern," I said, thankful that my thoughts were not audible; I didn't want my boss to know that the dead boy might be my father's child.

For the next ten minutes, I sat alone in my office. The sky was dark, the rain fell, and I wondered why this business with Danny Jones was getting to me. What if he *was* Daddy's son, I thought. It wouldn't be the first time this kind of thing had happened. Mama wouldn't leave Daddy because of it. Now that Danny was dead, the whole thing should have few implications for my family.

I picked up the phone, dialed word processing, and spoke to Mary, the supervisor. Satisfied that the Roebling brief would be typed before lunch, I decided to have another cup of coffee. I couldn't shake my nervousness, a gnawing feeling in my stomach. Thoughts tumbled back and forth, rationalizing, justifying, denying. I tried to force myself to concentrate on the Matthews case, but it was no use. I knew that Danny Jones' death was not the end of my family's problem. Something deep inside told me that it was the beginning.

Chapter Five

The next morning when I awoke, the rain was so light it seemed more like drops of mist falling than rain. I stood looking out of the window of my apartment, which gave me a view of a tree-lined jogging trail and, beyond it, the frequented Hairston Parkway. Everything seemed normal, but then the scenery blurred into the image of Danny's twisted and broken body that somebody had left to rot in the woods; it seemed permanently etched in my mind. "I wish I hadn't seen it. I want to remember Danny as the awkward boy I saw playing basketball," I whispered.

The sound of a car passing on Hairston started me thinking about my father. I hadn't seen or talked to him since Mama told me about his involvement with Danny; to be honest, I felt betrayed. Unlike my brothers, I had always felt that Daddy was special. I remembered the many times I had defended him against my brothers' criticism. I had to admit that he had been a bit hard on them, insisting that he was getting them ready to go into the military. I thought of how he wanted them to be strong, brave, manly. I heard myself groan. *Nothing like that awkward Danny*, I thought. And to think he offered a five-thousand-dollar reward for finding him. I wondered how he was taking Danny's death. The next time I talked to Mama, I would ask. The telephone rang. I looked at it and let it ring five times before I picked up the receiver. It was Cliff, the guy I'd been dating. "I'm glad you called," I confessed.

His voice was low. "You sound like something is wrong," he said.

"No," I lied, trying to conceal the collision of emotions deep inside me. "Nothing is wrong."

Cliff's voice mellowed. "Then you miss me, right?"

At that moment, I could picture the warmth of Cliff's smile and the clearness of his luminous eyes staring into mine and I felt a familiar surge. "You don't know how much!" I whispered.

"Then tell me," he said.

My spirit lightened. "More than you deserve," I said. "You're always running off and leaving me."

"I confess," he said. "But, I'm going to try to make amends."

For a moment he was silent. "Guess where I'm calling from right this minute?" he asked.

"I hope you're calling from your apartment or your

office," I said.

"Nassau," he said.

"Nassau…, the Bahamas?"

"Catch a flight and spend a few days with me."

Though the idea appealed to me, my mind rejected it immediately. "I can't do that," I said.

"Why not?"

"I've got a job and…."

He interrupted. "Sidney will understand, and the trip is on me!"

"Uhm," I said. "You've got a sudden urge to spend money?"

Cliff's voice trembled with excitement. "No, but my client does. I told Mrs. Webster that I missed you and she offered you a free trip."

"Where will I stay?"

"In her house and it's gorgeous. It's Mediterranean with a sweeping view of the ocean, which I might add is covered with a perfectly cloudless blue sky."

I objected. "Stop fooling around," I said, looking out of my window into the misty rain, which seemed destined to blanket the city for another few days.

Cliff ignored me. "I'm serious, Simone," he insisted. "Listen, the moment I saw this house I knew you'd love it."

I took a deep breath, then let it out. "Cliff, I can't leave Atlanta right now," I said. "I've just been assigned to a new case and…."

"Stop talking and say yes," Cliff said.

"I shook my head. "But Sidney and Mama…."

"I'll call Sidney and Mama," Cliff said.

"Oh no you won't," I said. There was a silence. I took a deep breath. I had vacation time coming, but I didn't think Sidney would agree to letting me have time off on such short notice. Then there was Mama; she needed me.

"Call Sidney, then pack your bags," Cliff said.

"I don't know," I said, hesitating.

"Simone," Cliff continued, "I'm trying to get you to come and enjoy some of my client's hospitality. You're the one who complains that I spend too much time out of town on business. I'm giving you the opportunity to share some of the fun of business travel with me."

"Sounds simple," I admitted, my resistance melting, "but you don't understand."

"Come on, Simone, stop fighting me," Cliff said.

"Cliff," I snapped, "what you say sounds wonderful, but I can't just jump up and leave my job. I mean, both Sidney and Mama are depending on me at this very moment."

Cliff chuckled. "I guess you're right," he said. "You're bright, intelligent, aggressive, and you write better briefs than most lawyers I know. To take four days off, totally abandoning the legal world and your mother, is unthinkable for you. It's okay; I understand. And, while I'm stretched out on white sandy beaches, swimming in clear blue water and enjoying Mrs. Webster's lava rock waterfall...."

"Please, Cliff," I said, my defenses crumbling, "try to understand this is just not a good time!"

"I understand," he said, ignoring my rationale, "but

please be advised that when I hang up this phone I'm going straight to the beach and...."

"That's enough," I said. I took a deep breath. "I admit Nassau sounds like the place for me to be, but how can I get a flight out of town so quickly?"

"I've got you booked on Delta flight 314 tonight at 11:30," he said.

I felt excited. "Cliff!"

"Be a good little lady and call Sidney this minute. If you must, tell him that I'm dying and that you have to come to save my life."

I shrugged as if I were being led toward the Bahamas against my will. "Okay," I agreed. "I'll call Sidney, but something has happened in Hampton."

"Tell me about it when you get to Nassau," he said, hanging up the phone.

I dropped the receiver on the hook and walked into the kitchen to fixed myself a cup of coffee. Half an hour later, I was in the shower, rehearsing my argument to Sidney. I had to convince him, I thought, that it was in his best interest for me to take four days off from work. It doesn't make sense, I thought. At nine o'clock I stepped out of the shower, dried myself, and put on clean pajamas. I put off calling Sidney by looking out of the kitchen window. It wasn't that I was afraid of my boss; it was just uncomfortable for me to ask for time off on such short notice without an emergency.

I heard myself imitating Cliff's argument. "There are times, Simone," he would have said, "when there is no logical reason for doing something. You want to go to Nassau and this is your chance to do so without it costing you one dime. Do it!"

I shrugged, walked over to the phone, and called Sidney. I hesitated, trying to choose my words. "Sidney," I started when I heard his voice on the other end of the line, "I'm wondering if it's possible for me to take the next four days off."

There was a silence. "Something wrong?" he asked.

"No," I admitted. "I just want to go to the Bahamas and spend a few days with my boyfriend."

There was another silence. "What about the Roebling pleading?"

"It's on your desk."

I heard him sigh and I held my breath. "Get Shirley started pulling background on Steven Foster and go and have some fun. It'll do you good," he said.

"Thanks," I said as I heard the phone click in my ear. I wondered if it would be that easy with Mama. I called her at her office. She is a social worker at the Department of Social Services. When I told her that I was taking a few days to go to the Bahamas, she made little comment. "What have you learned about Danny's death?" I asked, changing the subject of my trip.

"Abe got the preliminary coroner's report. Danny was killed by a gunshot wound to his chest."

"How long had he been dead?"

"Nobody knows. The coroner says that the heat makes it impossible for him to pinpoint the exact day and time."

"What do you think?"

55

"I think Danny was killed two weeks ago, around the time Lucy started saying that something had happened to him."

"Maybe Lucy killed him," I said.

"I don't think so," Mama said.

"I suppose you've told Daddy."

"Yes," she said. "He's sick about the whole thing."

"Is he coming home?"

"He'll be here for a few hours Saturday to attend the funeral."

"You sound weary," I said. "Are you going to be all right?"

"I guess I'm a bit worried about James, but for the most part I'm all right. By the way," Mama said, her voice taking on a mysterious tone, "there was something strange about Danny's body."

"Strange?"

Mama's voice dropped. "Danny didn't have on any shoes and there were none found in the immediate area."

I rolled my eyes. "That's strange?"

"To me it's strange," she said. "Strange enough for me to go to those woods and do some more searching."

I felt my hand tighten around the telephone receiver. "Don't go without me!" I said.

"You'll be away for a whole week," Mama replied after a long silence.

"I can come see you Saturday after next," I said. "You can wait until then."

She sounded determined. "Things might be gone by that time."

"What things?" I demanded.

"Danny's shoes, for one thing," she said. "And there may be other things Abe and his deputies overlooked."

"Mama, please," I said. "It's not safe for you to go scurrying out in those woods alone. Please wait until I get home. I promise I'll be there the first Saturday after I get back from Nassau."

Mama didn't respond.

I insisted. "Mama, promise me you won't go in the woods until I get home to go with you!"

Mama cleared her throat. When she spoke, her tone was lighter. "I guess I can wait," she said. "Whatever is left out there will wait for another week, if the killer doesn't go and get it!"

I took a deep breath and let it out. After a few more exchanges, we said good-bye, with me reiterating that I'd be in Hampton the Saturday after I returned from the Bahamas.

The next thing I did was to call Shirley and instruct her to send out several form letters requesting documents on both Steven Foster and Thomas Matthews, then I pulled down my suitcase and garment bag and began packing. At eleven o'clock that night, I was at Hartsfield International Airport, boarding Delta flight 314, headed to Miami.

Chapter Six

"From both the air and the ground, it looks like paradise," I told my parents. "It's a coral island set in a turquoise sea, fringed by white sandy beaches."

Five days had passed since I flew from Nassau. It was ten o'clock Saturday morning and, as I had promised, I was sitting in my parents' kitchen. Daddy was back from reserve camp and Mama had cooked a breakfast fit for a king. There was the usual bowl of steamy white grits, fluffy scrambled eggs, browned smoked sausages, crisp lean bacon, fresh peach preserves, biscuits, orange marmalade, orange juice, and coffee.

"Sounds beautiful," Mama said, looking into Daddy's face. She held a large serving spoon poised in midair, grits dripping off it toward her plate.

"Maybe one day James will take me to the Bahamas. We could use a second honeymoon."

I glanced across at him, trying to read my father's reaction to Mama's suggestion. His mouth was full of grits, eggs, and sausage. He swallowed, then took a sip of orange juice. He leaned back in his chair and nodded. "There are places in the States as pretty as any island," he said in his deep voice.

Mama finished serving herself and set the bowl down in the center of the table. "Did Cliff get any work done?" Mama asked.

"Yeah," I said. "The Websters finally worked out the divorce settlement."

Mama glanced up at me. "How long had they been married?"

"Twenty years, maybe more."

Mama picked up her fork, put some eggs on it, stuck it in her mouth, chewed, and swallowed. "I guess it's hard for the poor woman," she said.

"She doesn't sound very poor to me," Daddy snapped, his voice angry.

Mama glanced up, a startled look on her face. "I wasn't talking about her financial status," she said. "I mean, after spending the best years of your life in a marriage, it's hard to…."

Daddy cut in, his voice rising. "The man had a fling, something done without thinking, maybe some circumstances beyond his control."

My mouth opened in astonishment.

"If she wanted to save her marriage," he continued, "she should have understood, forgiven something like

59

that. Just because a man has an indiscretion doesn't mean he isn't a good man; he's still got character...."

I interrupted. "Daddy," I said, looking into his eyes, "I didn't tell you that Mr. Webster had an affair, but he had been going with his secretary for over five years and...."

Daddy's eyes shifted in Mama's direction for a brief second, then he began pushing eggs around his plate. "Marriage is forever, at least until death. If this Mrs. Webster believed in the sacredness of marriage and if she wanted to keep her husband like you said, she would have forgiven him and forgotten the whole thing!"

"I believe marriage is forever too," Mama said, her face calm and expressionless, "and couples should be able to work out their problems together...." She paused. "That is," she continued, "if there aren't any secrets between them."

I was relieved by the calmness of her reaction. Daddy refused to look into Mama's face, and I remembered an incident that had happened when I was about six, maybe seven. My brothers and I had been put to bed; I was half asleep when I was aroused by music. I crawled out of bed and crept into the living room, where my parents were dancing in the middle of the floor. I remembered seeing them wrapped in each others' arms, laughing, loving. Now, I felt a need for that past, a longing to see them look at each other the way they had that night.

"What's happening with Danny's murder?" I asked, the words coming from nowhere.

The sense of uneasiness thickened. Mama and Daddy glanced at each other, then Daddy reached for another biscuit.

"Nothing much," Mama said, looking at Daddy out of the corner of her eye. "I've talked to just about everybody who knew the boy and they can't think of anybody who would kill him."

Daddy laughed, a sound that came from deep in the center of his chest, and said, "It's just as easy to kill for no reason at to kill for a reason."

"James," Mama said, raising her eyebrows in an exaggerated arch, "that sounds so heartless."

"Haven't you ever felt like you could kill somebody?" The uneasiness intensified.

"No," Mama insisted, her gaze locked on Daddy's expression. "Being angry is one thing, but murder...."

He interrupted. "Murder..., killing, whatever you call it, after the first time it's easy," he said.

"I can't believe you don't find murder cruel!"

Sweat ran down Daddy's neck from his forehead. "Believe it!" he snarled.

"Maybe in combat," she said.

"Killing is the same," he said, his eyes unblinking. "Whether in combat or not, it's all the same!"

"James," Mama said, recoiling as if she had been slapped, "please stop talking like that. I know you don't mean it."

Daddy's expression hardened; an intense light seemed to pour from his eyes. "I mean it!" he snapped. "And stop telling me what I mean!"

My heart pounded; Daddy's mood was frightening.

"I remember hearing that a few guys who served in Vietnam were camping out in the woods near where Danny was found," I said, trying to ease the tension.

"So?" Daddy sneered.

Mama looked at me. "They're harmless," she said.

"Suppose," I said, "that they've gone nuts, you know, having flashbacks..., maybe remembering Vietnam. I mean...."

"I don't buy that," Daddy said.

"Daddy, some of them could be psychopathic!" I insisted.

The strange look on my father's face made me want to drop the veteran theory.

"Just because a man has been to Vietnam," he said, "doesn't mean that he's going around killing...."

Mama interrupted. "Eric says that Danny visited somebody in Savannah but he doesn't know who, although he thinks it may have been a relative," she said, changing the subject.

"Maybe it was like Rose said, an accident," I whispered. "A hunter who didn't realize that he had shot Danny."

Mama frowned, her forehead wrinkling in thought. She hesitated. "We'll find out who killed Danny," she said, her voice calm, "when we figure out why he wasn't wearing shoes."

I cleared my throat, was about to speak but then didn't. I couldn't think of what to say.

Daddy scanned Mama's face for a full minute, then he took a deep breath, stood up, and walked over to the window.

"Whatever happened," he said, his face anxious, "I've got to know!" He turned, walked over to the sink, and put his glass into the dishpan of soapy water.

"James," Mama said as he walked toward the door, "we're going into the woods where Danny's body was found."

Daddy grunted, then walked out of the kitchen.

I helped Mama with the dishes and, about a hour later, she and I were driving toward Camp Branch. It was the first of August, three months after I had first watched Danny play ball. It was ninety-five degrees, the humidity eighty-seven percent, and both were climbing.

My sense of apprehension grew as I followed Mama toward the clearing where Danny's body had been found. I glanced at the woods beyond; everything was quiet. There wasn't even the usual sound of some small creature foraging in the bush. Mama picked up a stick and began sifting through the ground cover. I stared at the ground surrounding her.

My chin quivered. "What kind of shoes are we looking for?" I asked.

"I don't know," she said, walking across the clearing toward a mound that had been pushed up by loggers. "It's just that Danny's being barefoot strikes me as odd."

"You know this is nuts," I said. "A few months ago Danny Jones was just a name. Now that he's dead, we think he was my father's illegitimate son and...."

Mama interrupted. "I don't think James is Danny's father," she said.

"I do," I said.

"You're wrong," she said. Then suddenly she called out, "Over here!" She was staring at the ground.

"What?" I asked, running toward her. Barely visible beyond the mound in a thicket of brush was what looked like a wristwatch. I moved closer, picking it up.

"It's James' watch," Mama whispered.

"How do you know?" I asked, my eyes glued to the watch in my hand.

Mama took a deep breath, filling her nostrils with the scent of the forest. "Because I gave it to him," she said. "I would know the watch I gave to my husband, wouldn't I?" She took it from me and turned it over. The inscription read: "To James from Candi."

I looked at Mama. "What is it doing here?" I asked.

Mama said nothing but stood there staring at the watch, frowning. Suddenly we heard the sound of a twig snapping, as if being trod underfoot. Mama dropped the watch. "Shh!" she said, holding her finger to her lips. "Listen!" It came again, a sharp snap, then another, followed by a rustling in the brush ahead and to the left.

Mama took a deep breath. "James!" she shouted. Nothing. We listened. "James, is that you?" she shouted again, this time with more force.

We waited, but there was no response. I felt a twinge of panic but put it down. "Who's out there?" I yelled.

Nothing. *A deer,* I thought. *It had to be a deer.* I touched Mama's arm. "It's a deer, and if we stand still it'll come out of the shadows so that we can see it."

I reached out to Mama. Together we stood, frozen, waiting. After what seemed an eternity, we sensed something close by, watching.

There was a faint rustling again as a shadowy figure crept closer. For a moment we stared, barely able to discern the shape from the surrounding shadows. The figure stopped and my blood ran cold.

I stooped, picked up the watch, dropped it in my pocket, gripped Mama's arm, and began guiding her toward the car. "Let's get out of here," I whispered.

When we reached the car, I locked the door. It was a full minute before either of us trusted ourselves to speak. Mama spoke first. "We're going back," she said. "We'll wait half an hour and then we'll go back."

"Why?" I asked. "Somebody is out there and it isn't Daddy!"

Mama glanced over at me but for a long moment said nothing. When she did speak, her voice was soft and grave. "Somebody is dead out there," she said. "When I took a deep breath, I smelled it!"

I glanced toward the woods. "I smelled something rotten, but it could have been an animal," I said.

"It was a human," she said.

"Then we'll get the sheriff!"

"Not now!" she said. "We'll drive to Varnville for a half hour or so, then come back."

"This thing is becoming dangerous."

"I've got to look in that area further," she insisted.

"Why?"

"Because I smelled the same odor the night they found Danny's body and, if there is another body out there, I want to see it first! In case there's something else…."

"We could get killed."

"Simone," she snapped, "has it occurred to you that, if James' watch was out there, other things of his might be there too…, things that neither of us want Abe to see until we get to the bottom of this mess!"

"Danny's death could have been an accident. A hunter shot him not realizing what he had done."

"Danny was murdered! And, when we find his shoes, or an explanation for where they are, we'll find his murderer!"

I turned the key in the car ignition. "Danny's shoes could be in a tree stump, put there by a squirrel or raccoon."

Mama leaned away from me, but I could feel her looking at my face. "If the shoes don't intrigue you, finding your father's watch in the same place that Danny's body was found should."

The words hung in the air between us. Mama seemed to be waiting for me to argue with her. I tried to think of what to say, but I couldn't come up with anything. All I could think of was that my father was involved in something, maybe something serious, and we had to get him out of it.

When I didn't speak, Mama continued. "Now, if James is in this mess, I want to find out about it before Abe does, and I'm not going to let any shadow in the woods scare me away!"

"Okay," I conceded, as I put my foot to the pedal and sped away. "I want to know what my daddy's watch was doing out there too but, if the person who murdered Danny was out there in the woods watching us, we could be his next victims." I swung the car onto highway 68 a bit too fast. We swirled toward an embankment.

"Keep your eyes on the road," Mama said, as I tried to keep from hitting the ditch.

"My heart is in my throat," I said. "I don't know if I could get used to digging up dead bodies and killers in the woods."

Mama eased back against the cushioned seat of my Honda. "If that person prowling in the woods wanted to hurt us, he could have. We're unarmed. I think he just wanted to scare us, and that's what I want him to believe he has done. So, we'll go to Varnville, get a Coke, and wait. After a while, when the person out there thinks we're gone, we'll go back and see if we can learn what it is he didn't want us to find!"

Forty-five minutes later, we pulled off the edge of the road, about a mile from where we had found the watch. We were hoping that the person in the woods had gone. But if he had not, he wouldn't see us approach. It took us a few minutes to walk to the spot where we'd found Daddy's watch. *Daddy's watch*, I thought. I patted my pocket; it was still there.

We stopped at the edge of the woods, making sure no one was in sight. We eased ourselves into the underbrush, crouching, listening for any sound that might betray the presence of the person who had frightened us before. Everything was quiet.

I surveyed the scene; we were surrounded by trees

with thick trunks and heavy branches. Mama began poking again, her eyes flickering back and forth from the underbrush into the woods. I struggled to swallow the lump in my throat and still my pounding heart. I noticed the birds, first as flashes, then as a congregation on the ground. Mama noticed them too and moved to the area where they were flocked.

The birds flew upward, and I agreed that the smell had to be the stench of rotting human flesh. Holding her nose, Mama took her stick and scattered away the leaves. Down in the underbrush rested the torso of a very young woman.

I stepped back, yet even as I did I felt myself drawn forward. It was something like curiosity, but I fought it by taking another step backward, then another, and when I had taken my fifth step, the feeling was gone, replaced by revulsion.

"Give me five minutes," Mama said, her voice confident, "then we'll go get Abe."

I didn't answer. My heart was beating in my temples, and it seemed like it took me forever to get to the car, open the door, and slump down inside.

Chapter Seven

An hour later, the sheriff and his two deputies were combing the woods, checking pine needles, blood, picking up anything that could be construed as evidence.

"Maybe it was an animal," I whispered as the bark of a dog drifted from somewhere in the woods. I nodded my head toward the sound, but nobody paid attention.

Sheriff Abe stopped to spit tobacco onto the ground. "Candi, you find anything interesting?" he asked.

Mama had another stick in her hands, poking through the underbrush. She seemed startled by his words. "No," she whispered.

"You think whoever killed Esther's boy killed this girl too?"

Mama nodded.

"Well, it wasn't poor old Lucy, 'cause she's still in Bull Street."

Mama looked at the sheriff for an instant and shook her head. "This girl was killed before Lucy was sent to Bull Street," she said.

He was silent a moment. "Lucy could have done it then," he said.

"I don't think so," Mama said, stepping farther away from where the torso had been found.

"The possums and coons ate the rest of her body," Sheriff Abe said, spitting again.

Mama hesitated, then stooped down to the ground to examine something next to a small stump. "I don't think so," she repeated.

Abe's voice was impatient as he pressed Mama for an explanation. "You know I'm always open to what you're thinking, Candi."

Mama stood straight up. "I know, Abe," she said smiling, "and I appreciate that. Right now, though, nothing comes to mind."

"Well whenever," he said, walking toward his deputies.

"We're leaving now," Mama said. "I'd appreciate you letting me know when you get the coroner's report."

Sheriff Abe waved his hand as if he was flicking a fly. Mama smiled again, then turned and motioned me toward the car.

"Did you find anything else?" I asked as we drove away.

"A button," Mama said. "A green button."

I got into bed early, worn out from the trek in the woods and the shock of discovering that somebody else had been murdered.

Sometime after midnight, I sat upright in the bed, my eyes opening wide, sensing that I had heard the sound of someone moving around in my room. For a moment I felt disoriented, then I realized that I was not in my apartment; I was in my bedroom at my parents' house. I snapped on the light. There was nobody in the room. I got out of bed, pulled on my robe, and walked out of the room toward the kitchen. I snapped on the kitchen light and glanced at the clock over the sink. One o'clock. I picked up the phone and dialed Cliff's number. The phone on the other end began ringing. On the eighth ring, the connection clicked and I heard Cliff's voice, his recorded voice. I hung up the phone and went into my bedroom, where, after tossing and turning, I fell asleep again.

The next morning Mama cooked another large breakfast. While we ate, she talked to Sheriff Abe on the phone.

"Did Sheriff Abe find any scars or birthmarks on the young woman?" I asked when she joined us at the table.

Mama shook her head. "No, but he estimates that she was about nineteen or twenty years old," she said.

Daddy ate.

"Abe said it's too early for the pathologist's report, but he said that it looks like somebody hacked off the girl's limbs with an ax."

"For god sake, why?"

"Sounds stupid," Daddy said.

"Sounds like a crazy is on the loose in those woods," I said.

"It's wasn't Lucy," Mama said.

"I wasn't thinking of Lucy," I said. "Maybe a stranger lurking in the woods. And we still haven't followed up on Crazy Joe."

"There's a connection between Danny and the girl," Mama said, ignoring my comment.

Daddy stared at her. "I know Danny better than anybody, and he never told me about a girl."

"James," Mama said, "what happened to that watch that I gave to you on our last anniversary?"

Daddy's eyes darkened, but he maintained his composure. "It's in the shop," he said, his words short and quick. "It stopped running, so I put it in the shop to get it fixed."

"Give me the receipt," Mama said, "and I'll pick it up for you."

"You can't pick it up," Daddy stammered. "It's on the base in Charleston. I'll get it out the next time I'm there."

Mama looked at me and smiled. I stood up and went to my room to search for the watch. It was not there. I sighed, picked up my overnight case, and walked to the kitchen.

"I'd better be getting to Atlanta," I said, looking at Daddy's expression. He nodded but didn't look up. Mama followed me to my car.

"What happened to the watch?" I asked. "It's not in my pocket!"

"Don't worry about it," she said.

"Did you come in my room last night and take it?" I asked.

Mama smiled. "Simone, forget the watch. I'll take care of it."

"But Mama," I said, "maybe it was Daddy in the woods yesterday. Maybe he was looking for his watch and maybe...."

Mama interrupted. "Simone, stop it," she said. "The next thing you'll be thinking is that James had something to do with the deaths of those young people. Just leave the watch to me and I'll take care of it."

"What are you going to do?" I asked.

"I've got a hunch," she said. "I'll call you later this week to tell you if it's a good one."

"You won't do anything without me, will you?"

"You mean get killed?" she teased. "I wouldn't think of dying without you." She kissed me and I drove away.

The normal four-and-a-half-hour trip took me almost six hours. I was exhausted. I couldn't dismiss the thought of my father being out in the woods trying to scare us away from a murder scene. Hungry when I arrived home, I opened a can of soup and checked the light on my answering machine. My girlfriend Donna had called.

Instead of returning Donna's call, I phoned Cliff. "Where were you at one this morning?" I asked when he answered.

There was sarcasm in his tone. "And how are *you*, darling?" he asked.

I repeated, "Where were you when I called you at one o'clock this morning?" my voice higher.

"I was at the gym," he said.

"What gym is open all night?" I asked.

"Run & Shoot in East Point," he said.

I took a deep breath, then let it out, struggling to control my embarrassment. "I'm sorry," I said.

"What's the matter with you?" he asked.

"Everything," I said, trying to swallow a lump in my throat.

"I'll be right over," he said.

An hour later, I had showered, put on my favorite house dress, an old white thing with pink and yellow polka dots, and was sitting on the sofa telling Cliff about the body of the dead girl that Mama and I had discovered. "Every time I go home and begin digging in the woods with Mama, there is a dead body!" I said.

"Does your mama think the dead girl has some connection to Danny?" Cliff asked.

"Yes," I admitted. "But that's not what is bothering me." I hesitated, not sure I wanted Cliff to know that I suspected my father of being involved in the case. Cliff waited. Finally I spoke. "I think my father is Danny's father too," I said.

"That's impossible," he said. "You told me that you are your parents' youngest child."

"I am," I said. "But my mother is not Danny's mother."

"You're pulling my leg," Cliff said.

"I wish I were."

"Your parents are the ideal," he said. "I've always looked at their marriage as the model, you know, the one that I want for us."

I nodded. "Me too," I said.

"Does your mother suspect?"

"She's the one who told me about the whole thing, but that's not the worst of it."

"There's more?"

"We found Daddy's watch at the scene of the murders," I said.

Cliff frowned.

"Somebody saw me pick it up and tried to scare us away. We pretended to leave but, about forty-five minutes later, we returned, and that is when we found the girl's torso."

Cliff rubbed his chin. "What about the watch?" he asked.

"That's what's got me scared," I said. "Last night I woke up thinking somebody was in my room. I got up and went into the kitchen." I looked up at him. "That's when I called you and got your answering machine," I said.

Cliff smiled.

"Anyway," I continued, "this morning, when we were eating breakfast, Mama asked Daddy about the watch, and he lied and said that he had put it in the shop on the base in Charleston."

"Did you produce the watch?"

"I went to the bedroom to look for it, but it was gone."

"You think your father got up in the middle of the night and took it out of…?"

"My pocket," I said, completing his sentence.

Cliff's mouth opened but no words came out. "I don't believe it," he said finally.

"I wish I didn't," I said.

"So you're telling me that you think your father has something to do with the death of Danny and the girl?"

"I'm thinking he might have killed them," I said, the words almost choking in my throat.

"For heaven sakes, why?"

"I don't know," I said. "There's no other reason for the way he's been acting."

"How has he been acting?"

"Well, for the first thing, he offered a five-thou-sand-dollar reward to anybody who found Danny alive. My father is the tightest man who ever lived and he would have never offered that kind of money unless he knew that Danny was dead."

"That's kind of a hard way to think, Simone," he said.

"It's true. From the moment Mama told me about that reward, I suspected he had more to do with this thing than met the eye."

"You know better than I do that's not enough evidence to convict a man for murder," Cliff said.

"Well," I continued, "yesterday when we were eating breakfast, Daddy went into this speech about how easy it is to kill and…."

Cliff interrupted. "Now Simone, you're being melodramatic. Your father is a retired military man; he has killed before."

"Well," I snapped, "what about the watch?"

"Now that's hard physical evidence, but it still doesn't place your father in the woods at the hour the murders were being committed," Cliff said.

"I know," I said. "But it's scary since he claims that the watch is in the shop when both Mama and I saw it in the woods!"

"When are you going to Hampton again?" he asked.

"I don't know. Mama said she is working on a hunch and, as soon as she sees how it develops, she'll call me."

"Let me know," he said, "because I want to go with you."

"How can I convince Mama?"

"Just tell her that you'll feel safer if a capable, strong man accompanies you two poor defenseless women," he said.

"I don't think so," I said.

"You do want me to come," he said, putting his arms around me and drawing me close.

For the next few days I didn't hear from Mama. At the office, I had begun working on the background information about Steven Foster, the man our client had shot while trying to break into his house. Steven Foster was a petty thief who had a record going back to high school. It seems that he always got caught while breaking and entering, the reason being because he was an alcoholic who was always over his limit

77

before his attempts. The autopsy report showed that he was pretty drunk the night of his death.

If Steven Foster was a failure as a burglar, our client Thomas Matthews was a bore. He was a tax consultant who had married into Atlanta's old money. Nothing exciting here, I thought, closing the folder. If my boss is going to get him off, he'll have to look beyond his history.

It was late when I left the office, after six. I remembered that there was nothing in my apartment to eat, so I stopped at Boston Rotisserie Chicken and picked up a dinner. When I got home, I threw my briefcase in the corner and tried to get Mama on the phone. I had an idea to try out on her, but there was no answer.

At eight o'clock, I was standing in the kitchen staring out of the window when the telephone rang. "Mama?" I answered.

"Simone," she said, "is something the matter?"

"I was worried about you," I said. "You haven't called in over a week."

"I'm all right," she said.

"You said you had a hunch; what happened?"

"I've got Abe working on it."

"Well, since nothing is happening on that end," I said, "maybe you'd like to come to Atlanta and spend some time with me."

"Why?"

"Well," I said, "It'll give you some distance from that mess in Hampton, and it might give you a new perspective."

"I don't need a new perspective," she said.

"Well, maybe you can help me here," I said.

"Are you having a problem?"

"I've got this new case," I said. She didn't respond. "I could use your opinion."

"You think this problem with Danny is too much for me?" she asked.

"I think you and I will feel better if we get our minds off the murders for a while," I blurted.

She was quiet.

"How's Daddy?" I asked.

"Quiet," she said.

"It'll do you both good for you to get away for a few days."

For a moment, she said nothing. "I'll talk to James," she said. "If it's okay with him, I'll come."

"It'll be good," I said, "like its supposed to be."

"I'll call you tomorrow," she said.

"Mama," I whispered, remembering her loyalty and conviction.

"Yes?" she said.

"I love you!"

"I love you too, Simone," she said.

Chapter Eight

I sat up in the bed in darkness, my eyes barely open as a ringing sound pounded my head. I reached for the clock: 5:00 A.M., too early. I was disoriented, but the sound that had awakened me was distinct. It rang again. I picked up the phone and spoke. "Hello."

"Simone, is that you?" a voice asked.

"I guess it's me," I mumbled, "I answered the phone."

"I've been trying to reach you for days. Girl, where have you been?"

"Here."

"Get up and put on the coffee pot. I'm coming over." *Click.* For a moment I sat there with the phone in my hand; then I put it onto the hook and went back to sleep.

The next thing I heard was a pounding on the door. I glanced at the clock: 6:00. "Not time yet," I mumbled.

"Simone, open the door," Donna yelled.

I lay still.

"Simone, open the door or I'll wake all your neighbors."

I hesitated, then got out of bed, slipped on my bathrobe, and answered the door.

"Girl, what is wrong with you?" Donna asked, brushing past me and heading for the kitchen.

"It's six o'clock," I said, yawning.

"I called, remember."

I rolled my eyes heavenward and gestured toward the bathroom. "Let me go in here, then I'll make coffee."

"You haven't made coffee yet," she grumbled.

The one thing I can do well is make coffee, but Donna couldn't wait until it perked so she stuck her cup under the drip pan and removed the pot. The coffee started leaking onto the counter, so I had to mop it up with a paper towel. I don't exaggerate when I say that my girlfriend Donna is a beautiful black woman. She has a flawless mocha complexion, bright slanting eyes, an altered nose, and full lips. Today she had on a black dress, a wide-brim black hat, and patent leather shoes with three-inch heels.

"You've got to come with me to Velma's," she said. "It's her annual sale!"

I shook my head. "There are more important things than a dress sale," I said, pouring myself a cup of coffee.

She tapped an acrylic nail against her cup. "Nothing is more important than Velma's dress sale," she said.

"Mama's coming," I told her, walking into the living room.

Donna followed. "So, bring her with you."

I curled up against a silk pillow on the sofa. "She's not coming to shop. She's coming to help me with a case," I said, clearing my throat and frowning. "And I'm not in a shopping mood."

Donna raised an eyebrow. "What's bothering you so much that you can't catch a dress sale?"

I began picking at my fingernail. "A boy was found murdered in Hampton a few weeks ago," I explained. "Not only did I see the body, but Mama and I had to break the news to his mother. Last weekend, Mama and I found the body of a young woman near where the boy's body was found, and we had to tell the sheriff; that's what's bothering me!"

"You saw two bodies in less than a month?"

I nodded. "It's the kind of thing that makes going to a dress sale unimportant!" I snapped.

She waved both hands. "I don't want to hear about it," she said.

"I didn't think you would," I said.

She grinned. "But I do want to hear about your trip to Nassau."

I shrugged. "It's a paradise," I said, my tone a bit softer. "From the moment I saw the island, I was sure that it had to be the loveliest place on earth. It's a green island, surrounded by a blue sea and white beaches. Mrs. Webster's house is built on top of a mound that overlooks the ocean. It's a twenty-minute drive from the airport. There is a private road, lined with trees and flowers. The house is about a mile down that road. I can see why she wanted to keep it."

Donna's pager beeped. She pushed it, noted the number, and reached for the phone. After a few minutes, she hung up and rose. "Got to go," she said. "You sure you don't feel like shopping?"

I shook my head. She patted her hair, then looked into her mirror. "Is your mama going to stay long?"

"A few days."

"Will she be cooking?"

"If she feels like it."

She closed the compact and winked. "If she does," she said, "Ernest and I will accept the invitation."

"What invitation?"

"The invitation to dinner," she said, opening the front door.

I nodded, then shut and locked the door. It was 6:30; the alarm clock went off. I finished my coffee, took a shower, and dressed.

Because I left my apartment earlier than normal, traffic on 285 wasn't as heavy. I stopped at the Nations Bank ATM machine and got some money for gas. By the time I reached the office, I had hit upon an idea.

I threw my briefcase on my desk and headed for my boss' office. Sidney was sitting behind his desk staring into the fireplace. His office is huge, with a large picture window, built-in bookcases, and an open fireplace. It has a large oak table in the middle of the floor, a huge oak desk, and a high-backed leather chair on brass wheels so that he can spin around the room to bookshelves or file cabinets. There is a black leather couch in front of the fireplace for intimate conversations with clients.

"I've got an idea," I said, throwing myself in the chair opposite his desk.

Sidney looked guarded. "About the Matthews case?"

"I want to talk to Mrs. Matthews."

"Why?"

"Maybe she can tell us something about the gun that Steven Foster had in his hand."

Sidney pushed back in his chair. He was silent for a moment, thinking things over. "What could she tell us that her husband hasn't?"

"It's a hunch," I said.

Sidney's eyes were quiet with skepticism. "You want me to arrange it?"

I nodded. "I want to take Mama with me."

He smiled and his shoulders relaxed. "When is Candi coming to town?"

"Friday," I said. "It'll be good if we can go to the Matthews home Friday morning."

He leaned in his chair. "It's okay with me," he said, turning and looking into the fireplace. "Maybe you'd better go with me to Matthews' hearing this afternoon. It'll help show you how much we need to pull a rabbit out of the hat on this one!"

I walked into my office, my heart in my throat. I had acted on an impulse and it had worked. The telephone rang. It was Mama. "I can't get away until Thursday," she said.

"That's fine," I said. "Sidney is making arrangements for us to visit our client Friday."

"What's this case all about?" she asked.

"I'll fill you in when you get here," I said. "How are things developing on that end?"

"I've got Abe checking with the phone company."

"For what?"

"I want to know if Danny made any long-distance calls in the last six months."

"What are you looking for?"

"The dead girl is not local; nobody knows her and nobody has reported her missing. My guess is that she's from out of town. I say Savannah because Eric said that Danny sometimes visited Savannah. If there is a number he called in Savannah, it might give us a name and address."

"Sounds good to me," I said.

"The telephone company told Abe that it will take a week or two to get the information."

I took a deep breath. "How's Daddy?"

"Silent, sulky, mourning.... What can I say? Whenever he does speak he says crazy things."

"Like what?"

"Things that I don't wish to repeat."

I paused. "He needs time to think." There was a silence. "Mama," I asked, "do you think that Daddy could be involved in these killings?"

Mama's tone was not as confident as I'd hoped it would be. "James knows more than he is telling and it scares me that he doesn't feel secure enough to talk to me."

It scares me that he might be a killer, I thought.

"However James is involved in this mess, we'll find out and we'll stand behind him. We're a strong family and we'll stick together!"

"Okay," I said. "I'll look for you Thursday morning, early. By the way, Donna wants to know if you're planning to cook."

"What do you think?"

"I think it'll do us a world of good."

"Then I'll cook," she said.

At 1:30, Sidney and I entered the courtroom. This was the same courtroom where Cheryl LaFlamme's trial had taken place. Today, Judge Arthur Baldwin presided.

The judge was cordial. There was no jury. This wasn't a trial; it was a hearing to decide whether there should be any change in Thomas Matthews' status. The judge, after hearing the evidence, could dismiss or grant a motion for a trial.

It was not open court, but it was interesting enough for a few people from the press to be there.

The judge rapped his gravel and asked if the State was ready. When he asked if the defense was ready, Sidney answered yes.

I squirmed in my chair. The prosecutor was saying that the State was prepared to show that Steven Foster was intoxicated and confused and that it was not his intent to rob the Matthews home. Our client, Thomas Matthews, had given a statement that, despite his calling out to Steven Foster several times warning him that he had a gun, Foster continued trying to break in. Still, the prosecutor argued that there was no evidence that Foster was armed or posed any danger to the

Matthews family. They requested Thomas Matthews be tried for first-degree murder.

Sidney spoke, his voice casual and confident. He quoted cases and precedents, then boiled his argument down to the fact that, in the exclusive neighborhood of Dunwoody, it would be hard to believe that Steven Foster was so confused or intoxicated as to believe he was entering his own home. He itemized Foster's arrest record, emphasizing that on many other occasions Foster had been intoxicated and attempted to break into other homes and business establishments.

Judge Baldwin frowned and waved his hand back and forth to stop Sidney's lengthy speech.

"Was Steven Foster armed?" Judge Fleming asked.

"No," the prosecutor stated. "There is no evidence that he had a weapon of any kind."

"Did he enter the Matthews home to remove any of its belongings?" Judge Baldwin asked.

"No," the prosecutor answered.

Sidney started to speak but decided against it. I felt myself shifting in my seat again as I noticed the white flakes showering onto his shoulders. The judge looked over his thick-rimmed glasses and stated that the trial would be set for October 1. I opened my mouth, then shut it. Sidney had less than six weeks to prepare his case, a case that hinged on whether an intoxicated man was an armed and dangerous thief.

Sidney was annoyed. "Permission to approach the bench, Your Honor," he said, cocking his head so that the dandruff flowed from his head onto the shoulders of his gray suit.

"Come up," the judge said. I couldn't hear what was being said because they whispered. I could tell though that Sidney and the young prosecutor were having a go at it. When Sidney returned, he appeared relieved. He smiled at Thomas Matthews, who stood showing white teeth and frightened eyes.

"Let me know what Candi thinks of Mrs. Matthews' statement," he said, closing his briefcase.

Chapter Nine

Whenever I am driving alone I listen to the radio station KISS 104.7. Today, I was not alone, so I reached over and pushed the off button. It was one o'clock Friday, and Mama and I were driving north on 285. We were headed to Dunwoody to visit Mrs. Matthews. I was telling Mama that the idea of visiting our client's wife had come to me out of the blue.

"It was a hunch," I said, "a hunch that I hope will pay off, because Sidney's got less than six weeks to prepare his case, and if we can't prove that Steven Foster had a gun, Sidney might have to strike a bargain with that young prosecutor in the public defender's office."

"And," Mama asked, "that would be bad?"

"Sidney never likes to bargain," I said, aware that,

of all the cases he had defended, he had won ninety-eight percent.

"I'm optimistic," Mama said, patting my arm. "Most of the right answers I've stumbled upon were from playing hunches," she said.

"Your hunches are good, but it's scary making a decision not based on logic."

Mama was grabbing my arm, gripping it. "Slow down!" she shouted. "You're driving too fast."

I looked at the speedometer; it was at seventy-five. I eased my foot from the gas. "Don't do that!" I said. "You'll cause me to kill us and somebody else. Besides, this is Atlanta, remember? You're expected to drive fast."

"Not with me in the car," Mama said, relaxing in her seat. She sighed and then returned to our previous conversation. "Your hunch might pay off."

I shook my head. "I don't like the way it makes me feel," I said. "But I have to admit I've got a gut feeling that Mrs. Matthews is going to lead me to Steven Foster's gun."

"You're right," she said.

"Still," I said, "you'd think that, if the gun is at the Matthews house, they would have given it to the police on the night of the shooting."

"They would if they knew where it was," Mama said.

"I don't even know what I have to ask Mrs. Matthews," I said.

"Nothing," Mama said, casting a smile toward me. "Just talk to her about what happened the night of the attempted break-in."

"What am I looking for?"

"Whatever is obvious," she said. "Answers are usually right in front of your eyes, in plain sight."

"That doesn't compute to my logical mind," I commented.

Mama smiled. "Look at everything we see and listen to everything that is said. Now," she said, changing the subject, "tell me again what happened the night Steven Foster tried to rob Thomas Matthews' home."

I had just finished the story as we were driving up the hill to a three-story brick house that looked like it could have housed three families. I stopped the car and took a deep breath.

"Relax," Mama said, patting my hand. "Think of it as just going to have a little chat with Mrs. Matthews."

A thin black woman answered my first ring. She was short, with a trim body, and something gave me the impression that she was wasting an education. She wore a dark blue dress, a sensible pair of shoes, and a white apron.

"My name is Simone Covington," I said. "Sidney Jacoby arranged an appointment with Mrs. Matthews."

She motioned us inside. We followed her into a hall that had a central stairway with a mahogany railing curving down to an ornate newel post. I could see to the right a living room, to the left a library, and straight down the hall another room that I could only describe as a study. The maid led us into the living room, which had walls a little darker than ivory. The drapes were pastel peach. The room was thickly carpeted and the furniture was upholstered in white satin. The low coffee table was marble. I assumed the framed pictures set around were family photographs. A fine painting of a black English setter hung on the wall over a beige marble fireplace. Over the sofa, on the longest wall, hung another large painting of a black setter. The house was quiet; the only sound was a clock ticking somewhere in the hall. Mrs. Matthews' voice startled me.

"What can I do for you?" she asked.

Mama smiled. "It's good of you to see us," she said.

Mrs. Matthews' eyebrows lifted. "Sidney Jacoby suggested it," she said. "Are you detectives?"

"No," Mama replied.

Mrs. Matthews spread her hands. "Then, I can't for the life of me understand why Sidney wished me to talk to you. At any rate," she continued, "won't you sit."

"He thought," Mama said, her body relaxing on the satin sofa, "that maybe if you could tell us what you remembered about the night of the attempted break-in, it would help him find out what happened to the gun Steven Foster had."

"I see," she said. "Would you like some coffee?"

Mama and I both nodded acceptance. She walked out of the room and I looked at Mama, but Mama just smiled. A few minutes later, Mrs. Matthews returned. "Meredith will bring the coffee in a moment," she said, seating herself in a white satin armchair.

Mama leaned forward. "On the night of the shooting," she began, "you must have been scared out of your wits."

Mrs. Matthews sat erect. "You have no idea," she said. "Thomas and I were in bed…."

Mama interrupted. "Do you remember what time it was when Steven Foster tried to enter…?"

"About three in the morning," Mrs. Matthews said. "I recall looking at the clock on my nightstand. Thomas and I were in bed," she repeated, "when we heard Leonard bark."

Mama's eyebrow raised. "You have a dog?"

"We've got Leonard," she said, pointing to the two paintings.

Mama nodded. "Leonard was barking…."

Mrs. Matthews took a deep breath. "Actually," she said, as if she remembered something, "Leonard woke me up. It was I who had to wake Thomas. You see, we'd had a dinner party earlier and Thomas had indulged a bit too much." Her voice was low.

If she didn't want Meredith to hear her admit that her husband drank too much, it was too late. Meredith walked into the room carrying a silver tray. On top sat a beautiful silver pot, three china cups with saucers, and serving pieces. It was the kind of china my wallet would allow me to admire but not to buy. We sat as Meredith served coffee.

After a few sips, Mrs. Matthews put her cup down on the table.

She was silent for a few moments, thinking things over. "Where was I?" she asked.

Mama's eyes were quiet and understanding. "Leonard woke you up," she said.

"Yes. It is very unusual for Leonard to be barking."

"You mean he doesn't bark?"

Mrs. Matthews looked at Mama. "Leonard has been trained not to bark except on command," she said.

I cleared my throat but Mama smiled, as if it was common for dogs not to bark unless told to do so.

"He was barking and running from one window to the other," Mrs. Matthews said, looking into my mother's sympathetic face. "After I woke Thomas and told him that someone was trying to get in, he pulled his gun from his nightstand and I followed him downstairs. The man, Steven Foster, went to the first window. As soon as we got to it, he moved to another. He moved around to five different windows until he found one that wasn't securely latched and...." She paused.

Mama nodded.

"Thomas began shouting that he had a gun and he would shoot if this man entered the house," Mrs. Matthews took a deep breath.

Mama smiled. "What happened then?" she asked.

Mrs. Matthews cleared her throat. "The man, Steven Foster, ignored Thomas' warning. The idiot kept trying to open the window. I screamed. Thomas looked out and saw the gun in his hand. Thomas shouted again, then opened the door and shot Steven Foster, he thought in the arm. I screamed again. Thomas came into the house and called the police. When the police arrived, they found the man dead."

Mrs. Matthews picked up her cup again and sipped. Mama did the same. Mrs. Matthews put her cup down and leaned back in her chair. "A week later, the prosecutor brought charges on Thomas, saying that he shouldn't have shot an unarmed man."

Mama appeared to think about this for a moment.

"This whole thing is ridiculous," Mrs. Matthews said. "That man was trying to break into our home. He could have killed us. There is no sane reason Thomas shouldn't have...."

Mama interrupted. "What did Leonard do during the attempted robbery?" she asked.

Mrs. Matthews' eyes widened in surprise. "For heaven sakes, why?" she asked.

Mama leaned forward. "I'm curious to know what happened to Leonard when your husband opened the door and walked out to face Steven Foster."

She shrugged. "Nothing happened to him," she said.

Mama now looked at Mrs. Matthews with great interest and I knew that she was onto something. "Did Leonard go outside with your husband?" she asked.

Mrs. Matthews' eyes narrowed. "Of course not," she said. "Leonard never steps outside these doors without me! Really," she said, "the whole thing was so stressful I must admit I forgot Leonard for a few moments, but believe me he never goes outside without being on a leash. It's just not done," she said with finality.

Mama leaned forward and changed the subject. "You have a beautiful home," she said.

Mrs. Matthews relaxed. "Thank you."

"Does the house reflect your husband's taste?" Mama asked.

"Thomas?" the woman laughed. "He'd just as soon

live in a house with walls papered green or brown. He's earthy, you know," she said.

After a bit more small talk, Mama stood up to leave. "Do you remember where Leonard was when the police arrived?" she asked, looking at one of the paintings of Leonard that Mrs. Matthews had pointed to earlier.

"He was sitting inside the library."

"Thank you very much," Mama said, shaking Mrs. Matthews' hand. "I enjoyed our wonderful chat."

"I hope that I've been helpful in getting this dreadful mess cleared up," she said, showing us to the front door. "It's taking a toll on everybody in the house, including poor Leonard!"

"You've been helpful," Mama said. "But, when your husband comes home, tell him to ask Leonard to show him where he has hidden Steven Foster's gun."

Mrs. Matthews' mouth opened. "Leonard would never touch such a thing!" she snapped.

"I think he has hidden it," Mama said. "And, remember, if you find that gun, Mr. Jacoby can clear up this mess before it goes any further and peace will be restored to your household, including Leonard."

"Leonard!" Mrs. Matthews shouted, leaving us to shut the door behind ourselves.

Chapter Ten

At two o'clock we were driving south on 285. I exited at Memorial Drive, and we stopped at Morrison's for a late lunch. At 3:30 we walked into my office and I picked up a few messages.

At 3:45 the telephone rang; it was Mrs. Matthews. "Miss Covington," she said, her voice icy. "Would you please come to my house?"

I hesitated. "Tomorrow?"

"Right now," she said, sounding like she was giving me an order.

I glanced at my watch, then winked at Mama. "It's almost four o'clock."

"It's urgent," Mrs. Matthews said, her voice a bit warmer. She hesitated, then continued. "Leonard has found the burglar's gun." Her voice was low and agitated.

"We'll be right there," I said, hanging up the phone. I laughed. The idea had seemed so absurd that Mrs. Matthews had been offended that the dog might have hidden the gun. "Leonard has given up the gun," I said.

I called Lieutenant Whiteside at the Fulton County police department and asked him for the name of the detective who had been assigned to the case. He switched me over to Lieutenant Harris Brown. I told him that the gun had been found and asked him to meet us at the Matthews house in forty-five minutes.

Mama was already at the door when I hung up the phone. I grabbed my camera, checked it for film, and then we headed for the car. It was so close to rush hour that it took us an hour to reach Dunwoody.

When we arrived at the house, Meredith led us to Mrs. Matthews, who was waiting at the top of the stairs. She in turn led us into the master suite, which consisted of a bedroom, a sitting room, and a bath. The sitting room had a red-striped Victorian couch, two straight-backed chairs, and a leather-topped table with fat legs. It stood in front of a window. Against the wall, opposite the window, next to the beautiful couch, was a mahogany desk. The gun was lying on the floor in front of the couch. Leonard was lying on the couch, obviously having been given a scolding.

As Mrs. Matthews led us into the room, her voice sounded in control, but I couldn't help noticing that her trembling hands told another story. "I had to get firm with him," she said, turning to look at Leonard while talking to us. "He's knows not to touch things without being told!"

From somewhere behind us, Meredith whispered, "That dog is always hiding things. It's what a dog's supposed to do."

"I'm going to punish you," Mrs. Matthews said, shaking her finger in Leonard's face. "Meredith," she said over her shoulder, "Leonard cannot have his treat for the entire week!"

Meredith leaned forward to peer past her boss. "When are you to going to realize that he's just a dog?" she said.

Mrs. Matthews glanced at Meredith but chose to ignore her remark. When she spoke, her voice dropped. "I've already called the school," she continued, looking into the dog's eyes. "As much as you dislike it, I must send you back."

Meredith grunted as if she knew that her employer was wasting her time. I smiled. Mama patted Mrs. Matthews' shoulder.

Lieutenant Brown arrived and took possession of the gun, promising to let Sidney know whose name it was registered in. We thanked Mrs. Matthews for subjecting Leonard to her interrogation, and then we left the premises.

By nine o'clock the next morning we had gotten up, showered, had coffee, and were ready to go to the farmer's market in Decatur, where Mama would shop for the dinner she was planning to cook for Cliff, Ernest, Donna, and me. Sidney promised to drop in later. Before retiring the night before, Mama had made up the menu, deciding on seafood: lobster, shrimp, red snapper, and oysters in the shell. She bought green cabbage to make cole slaw as well as a tossed salad. There would be homemade hush puppies. For dessert, she would make peach and cherry cobblers and a sour-cream pound cake.

"Mama," I said after we returned to the apartment, "I'm worried."

She was standing at the sink in my kitchen, peeling shrimp. "About what?" she asked.

I was sitting watching her work. "About Daddy," I said.

She stopped and stood silently for a moment, as if thinking things over. "I wish I could tell you that James is not involved in this mess," she said, "but I would be lying."

"Do you think he killed Danny?"

She shook her head and took a deep breath. "For what reason, Simone?" she asked. "James had no motive to kill Danny."

"Suppose Danny was his son and suppose Danny threatened to tell everybody that Daddy was his father?"

Mama chuckled and returned to cleaning the shrimp. "That's no reason for James to kill the boy," she said.

"People have been killed for less reason," I said.

"Then why would he kill the girl?" she asked.

"What makes you so sure that the two deaths are related?" I asked.

"A hunch," she said. "A hunch that might pay off when Abe gets Esther's phone records."

"Okay," I said, "let's say that Daddy had no motive

to kill Danny. That doesn't explain why his watch was at the scene of the murders."

Mama frowned. "And the button from his green khaki jacket."

"What?"

She nodded. "You remember the button I found in the woods?"

"Yes."

"It came from your daddy's green jacket."

"How do you know."

"I sewed it on a few days before Danny was reported missing. I remember because I spent several weeks looking for a match and I found one in Savannah. I recognized it the first time I saw it." She hesitated. "That is why I insisted on checking the area where we found the girl before I called Abe. I wanted to make sure that the jacket itself wasn't there," she said.

"Where is the jacket now?"

"James said he left it at camp but I don't believe him," she said.

"You haven't told the sheriff about the watch or the button, have you?" I whispered.

Mama sighed. "Of course not," she said. "I can't tell Abe about the watch, the jacket, or…." Her voice trailed off.

"What?"

"I don't know," she said. "I don't want to say any more until I know for sure."

"Mama," I said, "I told Cliff."

She stopped working at the sink and turned to face me. "You did what?"

"I told him about what's going on in Hampton, and...."

She interrupted. "Simone, you talked about our family secrets?"

"No, I mean yes," I said, feeling relieved that I'd told her of my conversation with Cliff. "What I told him was about Daddy's relationship with Danny and the watch and...."

She cut me off. "And I suppose you told him that you think your father is a killer!"

"Mama," I said, "I trust Cliff!"

She frowned at me, her eyes darkening, her forehead wrinkling. "So," she said, her voice turning to ice, "did you tell him that you think James is a murderer?"

I felt tears well up in my eyes. "It's just that I'm struggling to make sense of this whole thing and I needed somebody to talk to, and I trust Cliff!"

We gazed at each other for a moment in silence. When she spoke again, her mood seemed changed; she had regained her composure. "I'm sorry," she said, her voice again in control. She turned, rinsed the shrimp, and placed them in the refrigerator. She washed her hands. "I trust Cliff too," she said. It seemed like another minute before she spoke again. "What does Cliff propose to do about your suspicion?"

I felt a wonderful sense of release. "I'm not suspicious, Mama," I said, a bit more confidently. "I'm worried about my father!"

She reached for the cabbage from the refrigerator, walked over to the sink, and began grating it.

"He wants to come with me when I return to Hampton, in case...."

She interrupted again. "In case what?"

I slouched forward in my chair and took a deep breath. "In case we find something that might incriminate Daddy," I said, choking a little on the words.

Mama scratched her nose; her brow arched. "I believe we've already found some things that incriminate him, haven't we?"

"Yes," I said. "No..., I mean, you yourself said that Daddy had no motive for killing Danny or the girl." I remembered that my father was no longer the big quiet man who had once instilled a sense of calm and comfort but now gave evidence of a tension, as if a spring somewhere inside was being wound tighter and tighter.

I cleared my throat and sat erect in my chair. "Suppose Lucy killed them," I said, trying to sound judicious. "You said that she was not in Bull Street when both Danny and the girl were killed. Maybe that's why she's lost it, you know..., she couldn't handle knowing what she had done!"

"Simone, that is the most ridiculous thing I've heard yet," Mama said, rolling her eyes in disbelief. "If James didn't have a motive to kill those two innocent children, Lucy didn't have one either. What bothers me is why Danny didn't have on his shoes when he was killed!"

"Because he was an eighteen-year-old dummy," I snapped. "A dummy who got himself killed and got my father implicated in his murder."

Mama looked at me. "There's more to it than that," she said, her head cocked, her eyes fixed on my face. I squirmed in my chair; she was making me feel uneasy. For several moments she stood not saying a word. I had seen that look before; a tiny voice in the back of her head was sending out signals, signals that were giving her answers, answers that she was not going to share with me at this time.

She began smiling. I held my breath. When she spoke, her voice was low and even. "Suppose Danny wasn't as innocent as he looked," she whispered.

Chapter Eleven

Two weeks later, Cliff and I drove to Hampton together. We turned off Wesley Chapel Road onto Interstate 20 and headed toward Augusta, where we cut off toward Allendale and then on to Hampton. Mama's hunch had paid off; she had found something interesting in Esther's telephone records that Sheriff Abe had obtained from the phone company.

After the four-hour drive, we were welcomed at Mama's house by the smell of sizzling, popping chicken being fried in the kitchen. Mama was standing in front of the stove, adjusting the flame under the skillet. A glass plate full of seasoned flour sat on the edge of the kitchen counter.

"Thanks for cooking for me," Cliff said, as we entered.

Mama turned some chicken pieces over in the frying pan. They were mahogany brown with a spiced, speckled crust. "James will need to eat," she said, turning the burner up under the coffee pot.

I walked across the room to the cabinet and pulled out two mugs. Cliff went straight to the table, pulled out a chair, and sat. "Where is Daddy?" I asked.

Before I had finished my question, Daddy walked into the kitchen looking like an attack dog ready to spring. "Candi, what time will you be back?" he asked, sitting down at the table without speaking to me or Cliff. My mouth dropped open, but Cliff shook his head, warning me not to say anything.

"I don't know," Mama said, pouring coffee into a mug and serving it to him.

I got up and walked over to my father's chair, threw my arms around his neck, and whispered. "How's my favorite daddy?"

"I'm doing fine," he said, a slight edge to his voice that I didn't much like.

I hugged him again, then walked over and sat in my chair. "I suppose Mama has told you that she found Danny had another friend?" I said.

"Some boy he played ball with," Daddy said.

"I don't think it was a male friend," Mama said, putting fresh pieces of chicken in the skillet. "I called that number and talked to a woman named Trudy Pope and she said that no males lived in the house."

"Who lives there?" Cliff asked.

"Trudy and her daughter," Mama said.

"So," I said, looking at my father, "Danny had a girlfriend, huh!"

Daddy's eyes narrowed and he looked so angry it seemed difficult for him to speak. "The boy was too young to have a girlfriend," he snapped.

Nobody said a word.

Daddy grew angrier. "If he had a girlfriend, it would have been some girl around here…, some girl he went to school with!"

"Well," Mama said, eyeing Daddy the way she does when she's trying to neutralize his mood, "we'll know more about Danny's connection with the Popes once we've talked to Trudy."

"You don't need to be going to Savannah," Daddy continued, not looking into Mama's face. "You're barking up the wrong tree this time. Whoever killed Danny is not in Savannah…. He's right here in Hampton County."

"James," Mama asked, her voice soft, "who do you think killed Danny?"

"It was an accident," Daddy said. "Whoever killed him didn't mean to do it."

"And the girl?"

"That girl ain't had nothing to do with Danny," he said. "It's just a coincidence that she was found near where they found him!"

"Why do you say that?" Mama asked.

"If Danny and the girl were killed by the same person, why didn't they find the girl's body the same time they discovered his? I'll tell you why," he said without giving Mama an opportunity to speak. "Because she was killed by some crazy after Danny was killed!"

"She was either killed just before, just after, or at the same time that Danny was killed," Mama said, her voice authoritative.

Daddy's eyes darkened. "How do you know?" he asked.

"The autopsy reports show that both bodies were at the same level of decomposition," she said.

"The reports could be wrong," he said.

"The fact that they were both killed with the same gun can't be wrong," Mama said.

Daddy looked up at Mama now; his eyes did not blink. "Have they found the gun?" he asked.

Mama shook her head. "No, but bullet fragments were found in both victims and they were identical. When Abe finds the gun, he'll have his killer!"

The lines in Daddy's face deepened. His eyes shifted past Mama toward the window. "What kind of gun does Abe say he's looking for?" he asked.

Daddy didn't notice, but I saw Mama cross her fingers. "Colt 45, U.S. Army issue," she said. I wondered why she had fudged that answer.

"Abe got any ideas?" Daddy asked.

"Some," Mama said, "but it'll take him a few days to check them out."

Daddy sat quietly for a minute, then grunted, stood up, and stormed out of the kitchen without saying anything else.

I cleared my throat and whispered to Cliff. "He's not the father I've known all my life."

Cliff shook his head as if puzzled, then stood up

and walked over to the stove, where Mama was still cooking. "Can I have a piece of fried chicken?" he asked.

Mama smiled and nodded.

Though I had an uneasy feeling that Mama was not being truthful about the gun that had killed Danny and the girl, I wanted a mood change, so I said no more about the gun or Daddy.

We were driving down highway 278 toward Ridgeland talking about the murders in general when Cliff broached the subject of the gun again. "How do you know that Danny and the girl were shot by the same gun?" he asked.

"I just suspect that they were, and I suspect that it was a U.S. Army issue Colt 45," she said.

"Isn't that the kind of gun Daddy keeps by the bed in his nightstand?" I asked.

Mama nodded.

"You think it was Daddy's gun that killed Danny and the girl?"

"Yes," she said.

I was speechless.

"What else did the autopsy report say about the victims?" Cliff asked.

"Most of it was technical, but Danny died from a gunshot wound through his chest. The coroner thinks there might have been a struggle."

"The same thing with the girl?" Cliff asked.

"Shot in the chest, but there is no indication that there was a struggle."

"Did they find the other parts of the girl's body?"

"No," Mama said, "but they are sure they weren't eaten by some animal."

"Why?" I asked.

"Somebody sawed off the girl's head, arms, and legs," she said.

"Why?"

"I don't know why," Mama said.

"I don't understand one thing," Cliff said. "You told your husband that the two were killed at or around the same time. If that is the case, why wasn't the girl's torso found the same time as Danny's body?"

"Because it wasn't there. Somebody moved it to that spot the day Simone and I discovered it. The coroner did find some whitish fibers attached to the torso, from a sheet or bedcover. That suggests that the torso was wrapped up and moved from another location."

"Why would anybody want to do that?" I asked.

"The killer probably intended to dispose of the torso by chopping it into pieces and burying or burning it. But, for some reason, he couldn't or wouldn't do the same to Danny's body, maybe because Lucy was already telling people that something bad had happened to him. I don't know. I guess I'm speculating that the killer began to think that, if the torso was found near where Danny's body was found, Abe would suspect that the killer of both victims was one and the same."

"If Daddy's watch and the button from his jacket were found with the torso, it might look as if Daddy killed the girl and maybe Danny too," I said.

"Yes," Mama continued. "And, if James' gun was used, then...."

I cut in. "Mama, do you realize that you're proving Daddy killed those two people?"

"No, I'm not, Simone," she said. "I'm saying that it might appear to Abe that James is the killer if he found that kind of evidence against him."

"Then you don't think Daddy killed those two people?" I asked.

"I *know* that James didn't kill them," Mama said. "But somebody is trying to make it seem like he killed them, and that raises another issue!"

"And my stubborn father is helping the killer with his evil temperament, lying, and evasiveness."

"But," Cliff interjected, "you don't know that it was your husband's gun that shot the two victims, do you?"

"No," Mama admitted, "I don't know that and I won't know that for sure until Abe either finds the gun that was used or James comes up with his gun."

"Why do you assume it was Daddy's gun that did the killings?" I asked.

"Otherwise finding James' watch and the button from his jacket doesn't make any sense," Mama said.

"It doesn't make any sense either that there is a murderer in Camp Branch who cold-bloodedly killed two people and then tried to make it seem that my father killed them," I said. "You've got to remember, Mama, this is not Atlanta. This is Hampton County, a rural community where people aren't sophisticated enough to frame two murders on somebody else."

"I know," Mama said. "That's why it's being done so clumsily."

"What do you mean?" Cliff asked.

"I don't know," Mama said. "There's just something odd about the way the bodies were found, weeks apart. And it still bothers me that I haven't figured out why Danny didn't have on any shoes."

We were crossing the bridge into Savannah. "I hope," I said, "that your hunch is right."

Mama looked up. "Which one?" she asked.

"The one that tells you somebody is trying to make it look like Daddy killed those two young people." I said.

Mama's voice sounded hurt. "What you mean is that you hope I can prove your father didn't killed Danny and the girl even though you think he did!"

Cliff cut in. "Simone didn't mean that, did you?" he said, looking at me.

I slouched down in my seat. "I'm sorry, Mama, if it sounds like I doubt my father's innocence," I said. "but you told me that he wasn't a liar either. And we've caught him in three or four lies in the past few weeks!"

Chapter Twelve

Trudy Pope lived in a shabby two-bedroom house surrounded by a strip of brownish lawn a few blocks off Board Street. Because it took us an hour to find the house, it was early evening by the time we arrived.

We stood on a worn front porch. Cliff knocked.

"C-Come in," a voice ordered.

My nervousness and apprehension evaporated when Cliff pushed the door open and we stepped into Trudy's living room. Trudy was sitting in a wheelchair by the window. She was a big woman, very overweight. On the table beside her was an almost full bottle of Seagram's 7 and a pitcher of water. Facing her across the room from her chair was a huge color television set. Two chairs leaned against the wall. A faded blue sofa sat in the middle of the floor.

Trudy looked up from the image on the television and smiled, then gestured for us to take a seat. Mama and I sat on the sofa. Cliff pulled up one of the chairs from against the wall. Trudy clicked the remote control and everything was quiet.

Mama cut through my thoughts by introducing us and explaining that she had been the person who had called and talked to Trudy over the phone.

Trudy nodded. "I-I'm sorry you came all this w-way," she stuttered, "L-Like I told you over the phone, I-I don't know a Danny Jones."

"You mentioned your daughter might know him," Mama said.

"J-Janie," Trudy said, looking toward the window, "Yeah s-she might know him, but she's out of town."

"I bet she's a beautiful girl," Mama commented in a tone she uses when she's trying to defuse mistrust.

Trudy nodded. "P-Prettiest thing you want to see. Reminds me of myself when I-I was young, before this…." She looked down at her legs.

"How long have you been in that chair?" Mama asked.

"T-Two years and three months," she said. "I-It happened one night. I-I was riding with this feller and…." Her eyes shifted. "I-I…well, if it wasn't for J-Janie, I don't know what I-I would've done," she said.

"I'd like to meet your daughter," Mama said.

"I-I told you, she's out of town."

"How long has she been gone?" Mama asked.

"T-Three, four weeks," Trudy said, trying to conceal her worry. "I'm not worried. S-She'll be back. J-Janie always comes back."

"Then she's gone on trips before?"

"W-When it suits her fancy," Trudy said. "S-She ain't no child, you know."

"I'd sure like to talk to her," Mama said, her brow knitted into a thoughtful frown.

"W-Why?"

Mama hesitated as if she was searching for the right answer. "Because I need some information about Danny Jones," she said. She hesitated again, then seemed to make up her mind to go on. "And I believe that Danny is Janie's boyfriend."

Trudy laughed. "J-Janie ain't got a boyfriend," she said.

Mama spread her hands, a gesture meant to flatter. "If she's as pretty as you say, she's got many boyfriends," she said, "but I need information about Danny Jones."

"D-Did he have money?" Trudy asked, shifting in her chair. "If he ain't got no money my J-Janie don't know nothing about him."

Mama let out a breath that she had been holding. "I don't know if he has money or not, but I believe that she knows him." Mama said nothing for a moment, then prompted, "He's about eighteen, although his face looks younger, like a boy. He's tall, brown-skinned, has a black mole on the side of his nose, and ears that stand out from his head. He's from Carolina."

Trudy's lips curved into a smile. "O-Oh you mean that skinny boy from C-Carolina," she said. "Yeah, my J-Janie took up a l-little time with him but not much 'cause he ain't got no means," she said.

115

"What?"

"H-He ain't got no job," Trudy grinned. "'Course, every time he came he had money. M-My J-Janie wouldn't see him if he didn't have money."

I leaned toward the edge of the couch. "So," Mama said, "whenever he came, he had plenty of money."

Trudy nodded. "Sometimes fifty dollars, sometimes seventy-five dollars. I-I guess you can say he had money, at least enough for my J-Janie to take up time with him." Her voice sounded as if it was natural for Janie to take money from men.

"Does he call Janie on the telephone often?" Mama asked.

Trudy's eyes looked away; a faint smile curled her mouth. "L-Late at night, when his mama was asleep. I told you, he's just a boy." She paused. "W-Whenever he could muster up some money, he'd call and tell J-Janie that he was coming to town."

"Did Janie ever go to Carolina to see Danny?"

"N-Naw," Trudy said. "J-Janie wouldn't go see no boy like that. I tell you, J-Janie use to laugh at him 'cause he tried to act like a man. To my J-Janie, he was just a boy."

The phone rang. Trudy wheeled over to the table where it was sitting and snatched up the receiver. "H-Hello," she said. She listened. "N-No, she ain't here," she said. Trembling, she dropped the phone on the hook and turned to face Mama again.

"Are you worried that Janie hasn't called you in a few weeks?" I asked, trying to find out what Trudy really thought about her daughter's absence.

Trudy glanced at me and said nothing. When she spoke, the tone of her voice had changed. "M-My baby knows how to take care of h-herself," she stuttered.

"Something might have happened to her," I said.

Trudy's tone was sharp. "J-Janie ain't no child," she said. "You think my J-Janie don't know how to take care of herself? Before s-she was this high," she held up her hand next to her chair, "I-I taught her how to take care of herself. N-Nobody can hurt my baby 'cause I taught her how to handle h-herself!"

My eyes wandered around the room and came to rest on a table that held the framed picture of a pretty young girl who looked almost twenty. I pointed at the photo. "Is that Janie's picture?" I asked.

Trudy turned to look at the picture, and for a minute there was an uncomfortable silence. When she spoke again there was a bit more confidence in her voice. "That's my J-Janie," she said, her eyes sparkling. "S-She'll be back to take care of her mama!"

I let out a breath that I realized I was holding.

"Did she have money?" Mama asked.

Trudy's eyes narrowed. "E-Enough to get home," she said.

"Does Janie have a gun?" Cliff asked.

Trudy looked guarded. "W-Wait a minute," she stuttered, her eyes fixed on Cliff. "I-I don't know what my baby's got, but whatever it is, she knows how to use it to take c-care of herself."

"What was she wearing the last time you saw her?" Cliff asked, keeping his eyes on Janie's picture.

Trudy's eyes narrowed even more; her jaw tightened. "W-Why you asking me my personal b-business?" she said. "I-I thought you wanted to know about the boy from C-Carolina, not about my J-Janie!"

Mama's eyebrow raised in an arch. "I'm sorry," she said, looking now into Trudy's face. "Cliff didn't mean to get personal. We just want to know more about Danny's visit to Janie."

There was a loud knock on the door. "Trudy," a voice called, "can I come in?"

Trudy cocked her head. "C-Come on in, Jessie," she hollered.

A woman, about sixty with salt-and-pepper hair and a narrow face, emerged through the front door, a large black bag slung over one shoulder and several pieces of mail in her right hand. She ran her free hand through her thick hair. "Mailman's come," she said, looking up. She paused. "I'm sorry, didn't know you had company," she said.

"T-That's all right," Trudy said, waving. "G-Give me my m-mail!"

"Anything from Janie?" I asked, keeping my eyes on Trudy's trembling hands.

Trudy flipped through the few envelopes and let out a sigh. She shook her head.

"Janie's been gone longer than usual this time," Jessie said.

"S-She'll be back," Trudy snapped. "Y-You talked to that girl A-Angie like I told you?"

Jessie nodded. "Angie said that she ain't talked to Janie in weeks," she said. "She also said it wasn't her

118

that called Janie that morning and offered her a job."

"You asked B-Betty?" Trudy pressed. "J-Janie done gone on jobs with B-Betty before."

Jessie looked puzzled. "I talked to Betty and I talked to all the other girls that Janie hangs with, and nobody ain't seen or heard from her in weeks. Are you sure somebody called Janie and offered her a job?"

"J-Janie wouldn't lie," Trudy said. "She told me that somebody called and offered her a lot of money if she would do something and s-she was going to do what it took to get that money. That's what she always says when she goes away on a j-job."

"Maybe it was Danny," I said. "Maybe he told Janie to come to Carolina and he would give her a lot of money."

Trudy said nothing for a moment. "I-I tell you it was a woman who called my J-Janie," she said. "B-Besides, Janie wouldn't go meet that boy. H-He didn't mean anything to her. J-Janie was nice to him 'cause he had a few dolls, but s-she didn't like him or nothing. H-He was a boy; h-how could he get his hands on a pile of money?"

For some reason Mama decided to change the subject. "Did Danny bring anything other than money?" she asked.

Trudy hesitated. "I-I don't know what you mean."

Just then, Jessie walked toward the front door, her eyes fixed on Trudy. "Janie's been gone almost a month now," she said. "Something bad could have happened to her. If I were you, I'd call the police and report her missing."

Trudy's hand tightened around the arm of her wheelchair; her fingers dug into the padding. "I-I ain't calling no police on my c-child!" she said. "W-Whatever J-Janie is doing, soon as she gets finished, she'll be back to take care of her m-mama!"

Jessie hesitated, then shook her head and left the room, slamming the door shut.

For several minutes, everything was quiet. I opened my mouth to speak but Mama held up a hand to stop me. Outside, we heard sirens. *Police cars*, I thought. Trudy sat looking out of the window as if she was searching for some kind of answer to her daughter's absence. The sirens died away, leaving silence.

Cliff stood up and spoke. "Did Danny call here from Carolina the day that Janie left home?" he asked.

Taken aback by the change in subject, Trudy shook her head. "N-Naw," she stuttered. "J-Janie left after one of her g-girlfriends called her. S-Sometimes, when the money is right, J-Janie goes out of town with one of her girlfriends, but she always comes back."

Cliff and I glanced at each other; Mama smiled, a trace of sympathy in her eyes. "Janie has never stayed away this long, has she?" she asked.

Trudy shifted in her chair; her right eye twitched. Now she looked as if she was no longer trying to repress her fears, no longer refusing to face the reality that something had happened to her child. *Any moment now*, I thought, *she'll go to pieces*.

"N-No," Trudy said. "But s-she'll be back. My J-Janie knows how to take care of herself and I-I know she'll be back s-soon." Trudy's voice had a hopelessness that dredged up the memory of the torso lying in the woods.

Mama walked over and stood behind Trudy and began rubbing her shoulders. Nobody spoke a word. What could we say? We all knew that Trudy didn't believe her own words.

Chapter Thirteen

Shadows cast by the dark sky and bright moon danced through the fledging saplings and large pines. Thick underbrush spread along the highway as far as the eye could see. Intermittently, there would be a break revealing small cultivated fields of soybeans.

We left Savannah and went up through Ridgeland, where we took highway 278 to the crossroads of highway 68, where we took a left toward Yemassee.

"Where are we going?" I asked as we started out.

"To visit Rose Smart," Mama said.

"Does she expect us?" I asked.

"No," Mama said, "but there are a few things I want to know about Danny's relatives and she's the best person to tell me."

Half a mile down 68, we turned, crossed the railroad track, and continued driving toward the big cin-der-block house that belonged to Rose. As we pulled in front of the wide porch that fronted the house, I felt a vague sense of uneasiness. It was leaving poor Trudy alone, I thought. Somebody should be there with her when she gets the news about poor Janie.

Trudy's house, like most around, stood in the mid-dle of a soybean field, its back flanked by endless woods of pines. As I stepped out of the car and start-ed toward the front steps I looked across the field toward the woods. Something moved. I felt a chill. "Somebody's out there," I whispered.

"Where?" Cliff asked, looking beyond me.

I pointed toward the movement. For a moment, the three of us stood staring toward the woods where I had seen the figure of a man. The figure moved again, out of the shadows into moonlight.

Mama gasped, and I turned to look at her. The fig-ure moved again and disappeared. Mama began walk-ing toward the woods.

"Mama, don't," I said. "It's too dark to go out there."

She ignored me and kept walking. "What are we going to do?" I asked Cliff.

For a split second he looked confused, then he ran and opened the trunk of the car, removing the tire jack. "Get the flashlight out of the car pocket," he ordered. I obeyed, and a few minutes later he and I were run-ning about fifteen steps behind Mama. There was a sharp bark from somewhere in the woods.

I breathed deeply. "It's a dog," I whispered, switch-ing on the flashlight. Mama kept walking.

"It *is* a dog, isn't it?" I asked Cliff, who pulled me with his free hand.

"I hope so," he said, his voice sounding a bit choked.

For a moment, I felt disoriented. Mama had stopped at the edge of the woods. When we reached her, she pointed out a trail for me to throw the flashlight on the floor of the woods. To the right we heard a dog barking; to the left I felt something human very near. I threw the light but we saw nothing but tree leaves being rustled by the wind.

Cliff slipped his arms around me. "We'd better not go any farther, Miss Candi," he said.

"It's too dangerous," I said, my voice trembling. There was a sharp snap of a twig, as if it had been broken under a shoe, then another snapping twig, followed by a rustling in the brush ahead. I cast the light toward the sound. We saw nothing. "Mama," I whispered, "the killer might be out there. Let's go, please!"

Mama stared at where I was shining the light. There was a rustling of bushes, and then suddenly we saw a human figure. Mama began inching toward him, but the figure stepped out of sight again. Unafraid, Mama kept walking. I reached for Mama's arm and began pulling her to us. She snatched away and I screamed.

"Shut up, Simone!" Mama said, "Look!" She pointed toward a thick stand of pines. The figure was there but, as we started walking toward the trees, it again disappeared.

The skin on my neck began crawling. "Please, please, Mama," I begged, "let's go now!"

Mama stopped, then shrugged. Her voice sounded disappointed as she whispered. "Thanks to your yelling, he's gone now," she said. Turning, she added, "We might as well go!"

Cliff and I followed her out of the woods toward Rose's house. The warm night air flooded us with the scents of nature but I couldn't appreciate it because I was too busy looking behind me, watching and listening for signs of the man who was still lurking in the woods.

A few minutes later we were standing on Rose's front porch.

"What's going on out there?" Rose hollered, as she opened the door.

I swallowed, and Cliff let out a breath he had been holding.

Rose's large living room was almost twice the size of Esther's living room. It was covered with thick-pile navy-blue carpet. At the three windows that overlooked the front of the house were heavy powder-blue drapes, professionally tailored. There was a long blue sofa with several matching armchairs, a glass coffee table, and large crystal lamps.

Mama explained why we had been snooping around the edge of the woods. "I thought I saw a man," she said, "but, I guess it was an animal, maybe a deer."

"I was watching you all out of my kitchen window," Rose said. "It was Crazy Joe out there." She laughed. "I told you he combs these woods, but he's harmless."

Rose offered us a cold drink and we accepted. When she returned and began serving us, Mama asked. "How was the funeral?"

"You mean Danny's funeral?" Rose asked.

Mama nodded, then sipped from her glass.

"It was fine," Rose declared. "Esther sure put the boy away nicely, though I know she'll be paying for it for a good many years. She ain't got much, you know."

"I'm sorry I couldn't make it," Mama said.

"Your husband was there," Rose said, eyeing Mama suspiciously.

"I know, but I couldn't get off from work," Mama said.

"Esther had a lot of support," Rose said, leaning back in her chair. "It was one of the finest funerals this county has had."

"How is Esther holding up?" Mama asked.

"Fair," Rose said, "She spends most of her days down at the cemetery, visiting Danny."

"Will Lucy be coming home soon?" I asked.

"I don't know," Rose admitted. "Esther hasn't been able to go to Columbia to see the poor woman. What with one thing after another...."

"So Lucy doesn't know about the killings?"

"Don't think so," Rose said. "Who's to tell her."

"How long have you known Esther and Lucy?" Mama asked.

"We were girls together."

"Do you think that Lucy could have killed Danny and the girl they found in the woods?" Cliff asked.

126

"Heavens no," Rose answered. "She's as nervous as a cat, scared to wring a chicken's neck. Believe me, Lucy ain't got a murderous spirit."

"What about their parents?" Mama asked, redirecting the conversation again.

"You mean the Joneses?" Rose answered. "They took the girls in when both parents died and nobody else in the family wanted them."

"How did the Joneses die?" Mama asked.

"Old age, I guess," Rose said. "I was up north at the time, but folks said they died within two weeks of each other. The thing about the Joneses is that they stayed pretty much to themselves."

"There was nothing strange about their deaths?" Mama asked.

"Not that I know of. They were old people, it was just their time to die."

"This is the second nervous breakdown for Lucy, isn't it?" Mama asked.

Rose nodded.

Mama decided to broach another subject. "Rose," she said, leaning forward, "did Esther ever tell you that Danny had a girlfriend in Savannah?" Mama asked.

Rose's eyes darted back and forth between us. "Are you kidding?" she said. "Esther wouldn't let that boy have no girlfriend!"

"Did Lucy ever mention Danny having a girlfriend?"

Rose didn't answer. She stood up, walked over to the window, and looked out into the darkness. Mama glanced toward me but didn't say anything.

"Listen," Rose said, staring out of the window, her voice low as if she didn't want anybody to hear what she was about to say, "if I tell you all something, you promise not to tell Esther?"

"We won't mention it again," Mama promised.

Rose's rutabaga complexion became flushed. "Esther would kill me if she found out what I've done," she said.

We promised.

She turned to look at us. "Danny looked young, but he was almost eighteen, you know," she said.

We nodded.

"He was a good boy, helped me around the place as much as he could." She hesitated. "I couldn't give him much money, being on a fixed income and all, so...."

"Go on," Mama prodded.

Rose took a deep breath. "So, a few times I let him use my car, and I think he drove into Savannah to see a girl. I don't know for sure," she said, "but I think that's where the boy went."

"Did he ever mention a girl named Janie Pope?" Mama asked.

"No," Rose said. "He never mentioned any girl; he just said that he went into town to have a little fun, that's all."

"Where was Esther?" Cliff asked.

"Staying with old people."

"What?" I asked.

"Esther moved to Ridgeland to take care of a sickly white woman. When the woman died Esther came home. Since then, anytime some white folk needs a person to sit with their sick for a night or two, they call Esther. That's how she makes her living. Whenever Danny knew that she would be sitting all night, he would ask me to use my car and, well, I let him. The boy was almost grown; he needed to get out with young people his age, and he always brought my car back in good condition, filled with gasoline."

Mama stood up and looked at her watch. "It's almost ten," she said, "we'd better be shoving on home."

Rose followed us to the door. "Come any time," she said as we walked out onto the porch.

"We will," Mama promised. "We'll be back to see you again, soon."

The moon was so bright it was almost as clear as day outside. I made a complete circle of the horizon with my eyes, taking in both the soybean field and the woods behind us. My flesh shivered. *Something*, I thought, *somebody is out there watching, waiting, and killing*.

Chapter Fourteen

It was midnight. We were in my parents' kitchen. Mama had made a pot of coffee, and I was slicing a deep yellow lemon-glazed pound cake. Daddy walked into the kitchen. He stood at the door for a moment, then, as if on second thought, he sat at the table. Mama smiled, poured him a cup of coffee, and motioned me to give him a piece of cake. A few minutes later, the four of us were drinking coffee and eating cake. Nobody said a word. I watched my father. He is about five-feet ten or eleven and has rugged looks that tell you he's a man who has spent most of his life outdoors.

Mama spoke first. "James," she said, her voice resolute, "we've been waiting to talk to you!"

"About what?" he asked, fumbling with his fork.

"I want to know why you were lurking in the woods

in back of Rose's house tonight," she said.

Cliff and I dropped our jaws, but we said nothing.

Daddy's voice was rigid, controlled. "Candi," he said, "what are you talking about?"

"James," Mama said, her voice tight, "I saw you in the woods behind Rose's house tonight!"

Daddy tried to smile, but it turned out a frown. "I don't know what you're talking about," he said.

I was confused. "I thought it was Crazy Joe," I stuttered.

"For heaven sakes, Simone," Mama snapped, "if I thought that it was Crazy Joe in those woods and not your father, do you think I would have gone out there?"

Daddy stood up and started around the corner of the table toward Mama, but she held her hand up to stop him. He paused. "Why, James?" she asked.

Daddy stood there, neither moving nor speaking.

Mama's hands spread in a helpless gesture, "James, it's time to stop playing games and tell us what's going on," she said.

Daddy looked as if he was trying to swallow a lump in his throat. He turned and sat down. Then, as if his resistance had finally crumbled, he took a deep breath and, letting it out, said, "I was looking for my jacket," he said.

I stood up so quickly that I bit my lip; I could taste the blood. My father was a stranger.

Daddy's voice dropped. "Let me explain," he said.

Cliff spoke. "Listen, Mr. Covington," he said, "I'm a lawyer...."

Daddy interrupted. "A divorce lawyer!"

"Still," Cliff continued, "it might be wise if you don't say anything until you hire a defense lawyer and…"

Daddy's eyes narrowed. "A defense lawyer!" he shouted, his pent-up emotions breaking free. "I don't need a defense lawyer because I haven't done anything that I need to be defended against!"

"James," Mama said, her voice as calm as possible, "you don't understand. Two people have been murdered in the area where you have been looking for your jacket."

"So what?" Daddy snapped, his eyes fixed on Mama's face. "I lost my jacket in the woods; is that a crime?"

"It's not a crime," Mama said, "but it doesn't make any sense."

I reached out and touched my father's hand; I could feel tears in my eyes. Daddy's evasiveness was giving me an uncomfortable feeling. "Please, Daddy," I begged, "we've already found your watch near where the girl's body was found."

Daddy leaned in his chair. "Okay," he admitted, "I was looking for my jacket and my watch and…." His voice trailed off.

Everything was quiet for a moment, as if each of us was trying to think of something to say. Mama spoke. "And what?" she said.

Daddy's face had a strange look to it, something close to but not fear, maybe apprehension tinged with perplexity. "And nothing," he said. "I was looking for my watch and jacket, that's all!"

"How did your watch and jacket get into the woods?" Mama asked.

"Danny had them," he said.

I cut in. "Did he steal them?" I asked.

"No," he admitted, his eyes fixed on Mama. "I loaned them to him."

"Why?" Mama asked.

Daddy's eyes shifted toward me. "He wanted to borrow them," he said.

Mama said nothing for a moment. I sat, turning Daddy's words over in my mind. Mama spoke. "You loaned an eighteen-year-old boy the eight-hundred-dollar watch I gave you as an anniversary gift?" she said.

"Candi, you don't understand," he said, looking at Mama, then turning away.

Mama's expression darkened. "I guess I should understand that you thought quite a bit of that boy, perhaps more than you thought of an expensive anniversary gift."

Cliff's brow rose. "Wait a minute," he interrupted. "We're about to get away from what is important right now."

"You're right," Mama said, regaining her composure.

"If the police knew that certain items were found on the scene that can prove Daddy was there...."

Daddy stared at Cliff; this time he looked scared. "What do you mean prove I was there?" he asked.

I stood up and began pacing the floor.

"I mean," Cliff said, "that if the police knew that your watch and jacket were left in the area where Danny and the girl's body were found and if they could establish that you were in the area that night, they might conclude...."

Mama had calmed down. "James, tell me the truth. Why were you looking for your things in those woods?" she asked again.

"Because I gave them to Danny."

"When was the last time you talked to Danny?" Mama asked.

"June fifth," Daddy said, his voice taut.

"Simone, sit," Mama ordered. I opened my mouth but no words came out. Cliff looked at me as I pulled my chair out from the table and sat down.

"You saw Danny on the fifth of June?" Cliff asked.

"That's what I said, isn't it?" Daddy snapped. He looked at Mama. "That's why I offered the reward," he said, his voice low. "I wanted somebody to say that they had seen Danny after I met him in the woods that night."

"Tell us what happened that night," Mama said.

"I don't remember much," he said.

"What?"

Daddy slumped in his chair. "The boy was young, you know, innocent. Anyway, he was having the usual adolescent problems and I was trying to help him. He liked talking to me and, well, I had given him my job number to call me if he needed me. A couple of times he did call and we arranged to meet in the clearing in the woods behind his house."

"Which clearing?"

"The one where the bodies were found," Daddy said.

"What happened on June fifth?"

"Danny called me at work and said he needed money."

"You gave him money that night?" I asked.

"The boy didn't have anybody except me," he said. "Nobody...."

"Go on," Mama said.

"That's it," Daddy said. "I met him, gave him money, and left."

Mama stared at Daddy but didn't say anything.

"Candi," Daddy said, his voice pleading, "try to understand; the boy needed me."

We sat, looking into my father's face. There was no trace of arrogance left, nothing of the coldness he had displayed earlier. Daddy's relationship with Danny made some sense. What he seemed to have gotten from the boy was the feeling of being needed.

Mama's voice sounded choked. "Did anything unusual happen the night you saw Danny?" she asked.

Daddy tilted his head and closed his eyes. "No," he said.

"When did you start worrying that something might have happened to Danny?" she asked.

"I don't know," he said, his eyes still closed, "I guess when Lucy started saying that something had happened to the boy. And I hadn't heard from him in a couple of days. I don't know."

"Who do you think killed Danny?" Cliff asked.

"I don't know. He was a kid; he couldn't have done anything that would warrant being killed and left out in the woods that way."

"Did you find the jacket?" I asked.

Daddy shook his head. "Neither the jacket nor the watch."

"I have the watch," Mama said.

I cut in. "It was you who slipped into my bedroom and took the watch out of my jacket pocket?"

"I wanted you to think that your father had taken it so you wouldn't mention finding it to anybody," she said.

"Did you find the jacket?" Daddy asked, opening his eyes.

"Only a button from it," she said.

"The squirrels or raccoons must have dragged it off," I said.

"Why didn't you tell us about the watch and jacket?" Mama asked.

"Because I didn't want you to think I had anything to do with this mess, and...." Again Daddy's voice trailed off.

Mama changed the subject. "Did Danny tell you that he knew a girl named Janie Pope who lived in Savannah?" she asked.

Daddy shook his head, but he didn't comment.

"Daddy, somebody killed Danny and Janie, and if Sheriff Abe knew that you saw Danny the night of June sixth and that your watch and the button from your jacket were found in the clearing, it might appear as if you killed those young people."

"Why would I want to kill them?" he whispered.

"It could be reasoned that, when you met Danny in the woods, Janie was with him. Danny had on your jacket, your watch. An argument occurred. You accused him of stealing from you. There was a struggle, you shot him and then panicked and shot Janie," I said.

"That's not true," Daddy said, his voice so low I could hardly hear him. "That can't be true," he said.

Mama cut her eyes at me. "Did Danny have on shoes that night?" she asked.

"Of course," Daddy answered.

"I wonder why he wasn't wearing shoes when his body was found," she mused.

Cliff and I glanced at each other.

Daddy got up from the table, stretched, then moved toward the door.

"James," Mama said, her voice strong, "what happened to your gun?"

Daddy turned; his eyes pleaded. He started to speak but changed his mind. Instead, he shook his head, then turned and walked out of the kitchen.

I looked into Mama's eyes and frowned; we both knew that my father was still withholding the complete truth about what had happened the night of June fifth.

Chapter Fifteen

On Sunday night, when Cliff and I arrived at my apartment, there were three messages on my answering machine, all from a woman named Meredith Black. At first I didn't recognize the name. However, after I had sent Cliff home, unpacked, and got settled, it was ten o'clock, but I dialed her number. When I heard the voice on the other end, I remembered who Meredith was. She was Thomas Matthews' housekeeper....

"I want to thank you for calling me back," she said, her voice singsong.

I frowned. "What's the problem?" I asked.

"I want to talk to you," she said. "Maybe we can have a meal together."

"When?" I asked.

"Whatever you say," she said.

"Noon tomorrow?" I suggested.

"That's fine with me, my dear. Where should we meet?"

"Stop by the office, Jacoby & Associates off Peachtree and Lenox. Do you know the area?"

"Downtown?"

"That's it," I said, clearing my throat. "I'll see you then."

When I turned off the lights and crawled into my bed, it was after midnight. I drifted into sleep and into dream. At first there was darkness, then I was walking in a nature preserve of sycamores, maples, and pines. There were birds, rabbits, deer, raccoons, and possums. There was a dog sitting at the edge of the forest, a large white collie, but he didn't bark. I was standing in an orchard of apple trees. I noticed a few birds were in the trees, but then birds seemed everywhere, moving restlessly from tree to tree, crowing as if they were arguing with one another. I turned to run, but the dog was sitting in the middle of the road. Two birds flew close beside me. I waved my arms. The birds gave a cry, then swooped past my head again. The dog came toward me, the birds swooped closer, and I heard myself scream twice. I woke up.

It was another two hours before I could go back to sleep and it was six o'clock the next morning when I awoke, the nightmare still very vivid in my mind. Almost as exhausted as I had been before bed the previous night, I showered and dressed and headed for work. Monday morning traffic was heavy on 85, most of it inbound, heading in my direction. Clouds lay across the city like a blanket, making the air warm and humid. The whole city felt like a greenhouse.

My office window faced south, looking out of the front right-hand corner of our building on Peachtree Street. If I stared out at a particular angle I could see the 85. Sometime after ten, I piled a few case files and transcripts on my desk and around my computer and spent the next two hours staring out of the window, watching the ebb and flow of traffic as people arrived at their offices. But I was not thinking about them; I was trying to figure out what had happened to Danny and the girl and what had been my father's part in the whole mess. Mama had convinced me that he hadn't killed the two, yet he had some connection with their murder. But what? It was so out of character for him to want to help Danny. Men or boys, he had said many times, don't need help; they need courage, fortitude, conviction, strength!

I closed my eyes and saw the look on my father's face as he admitted that he had been crawling around the woods, looking for his watch and jacket, and I felt sorry for him. The proud mask was gone; he needed help and he didn't know how to ask for it.

I thought about Mama and how she looked when she had confronted Daddy. She had touched her chin with her fingertips, shocked, and for a minute her face had seemed open so that we could all look inside and see her bewilderment and fear. There had been a quick flicker of concern, and then a glance at Daddy that had a depth of love that I don't know if he could understand. "Your dad was trying to help Danny by giving him money and letting the boy borrow his things," she had said.

Cliff and I had discussed this on our way to Atlanta. "It's strange," I said, "how Daddy became so attached to Danny yet was so distant with his own boys."

"He realizes how much of his boys' childhood he missed," Cliff suggested.

"I can see them all now," I said. "My father drilling them, determined to make them combative."

"He thought he was doing the right thing," Cliff said.

"I suppose, if you get right down to it, he snatched their innocence from them."

"Well, your father can be proud of them now," he said.

"You think that because both have become military career men, but still...."

Cliff interrupted. "I guess it doesn't make up for the loss of being needed. Your father did say that he felt Danny needed him, remember?"

I took a deep breath, then let it out. "Whatever need my brothers had for both my parents has been lost to their loyalty to Uncle Sam," I said.

"And your father knows that and feels responsible for it."

"Daddy should have encouraged Danny to go into the military; it might have helped him."

"At least it would have gotten him out of Camp Branch," Cliff said.

"Uncle Sam will teach you responsibility, teach you how to become a man," I said, mimicking the tone of my father's voice.

"You said that disdainfully," Cliff said.

"I said it the way I remember my father repeating it over and over again to my brothers while they stood at attention, looking into his eyes."

"Your father wasn't that bad and, if he was, he was doing what he thought was right, and that counts for something."

"I know," I admitted. "My father is a pretty nice guy. He was good to me and I remember, whenever he came home, he always brought us presents from all over the world, wherever he had been stationed. There were a lot of good times, secure times. Still...."

"What?"

"I can't help but wonder why Daddy gave Danny money."

Cliff glanced at me, a quizzical look on his face. He winked. "After your mama gets your daddy out of this mess, we'll ask him," he said.

I changed the subject. "I wonder why Danny never told Daddy about Janie Pope," I said.

There was a brief silence, as if Cliff was thinking it over. "Maybe he was afraid to tell him," he said. "Maybe he thought your father wouldn't like the idea of him seeing a girl like that."

"But Danny didn't tell Rose either," I said. "I can't imagine him being so secret about the first girl in his life, not mentioning it to the only two people he did open up to and talk with."

142

Cliff glanced into the rearview mirror, put on his signal light, and guided the car toward the left lane of the highway.

"Remember how Trudy Pope sat staring out of the window as we walked away," I said. "Didn't you want to tell her that Janie was dead?"

"The dead girl hasn't been identified yet," he said.

"I know," I replied. "The missing parts of her body haven't been found yet."

Neither Cliff nor I said much more for the rest of the drive to Atlanta. The thought passed through my mind that maybe my father knew about Janie but denied it so that he wouldn't be suspected of a double murder.

"Do you think my father is capable of killing?" I asked Cliff as he pulled up in front of my apartment complex.

The question caught him by surprise; he reached out and touched my hand. "I don't know," he said.

"He served three times in Vietnam," I said. "I guess he's killed before!"

Now, as I sat looking out onto highway 85, my words were ringing in my ears. "*He's killed before.*" I began scribbling with a pencil and a pad. "Who killed Danny Jones?" I whispered as I wrote in large letters. "Who killed Janie Pope?" The telephone on my desk rang. It was Lilly, the receptionist.

"Meredith Black is out here to see you," she said.

"Thanks." I hung up the phone, reached for my shoulder bag, and went off to my luncheon date.

Twenty minutes later, Meredith and I were sitting inside Red Lobster, looking over the menu.

"How did you find me?" I asked her, after deciding what I was going to eat.

"My dear," she said, there aren't that many Covingtons in the phone book, and I found a listing with the first name of Simone. So I took the chance and called."

I smiled. The waitress appeared and we ordered. I was about to ask Meredith what was on her mind when the two people sitting at a table across from ours began arguing. The waitress was standing at their table, but they kept arguing as if she wasn't there, or didn't matter.

"Is this your day off?" I asked, trying to get Meredith's attention. She was staring pointedly at the bickering couple.

Meredith nodded but did not break her stare. "My dear," she whispered, "I've found that, if you stare at them long enough, they'll get up and leave."

She was right. Even though the argument was growing nastier, the couple couldn't take Meredith's hawkeye stare, so they got up and walked out of the restaurant.

Both Meredith and I leaned back in our seats and laughed.

I had her attention. "What can I do for you, Meredith?" I asked.

Meredith considered for a moment, then flashed a deep and wide smile that transformed her whole face. Dimples cut into her cheeks, and her exotic eyes were full of light. She leaned forward. "My dear," she said straight, "you can help me find another job!"

I laughed. "So that's what this is all about."

She nodded. "You see," she said, "when I first came to Atlanta, I was told that to get an office job, I needed more training, you know, more than I had gotten in my country, where I had worked as a secretary in banking."

"Where is your country?" I asked.

"The Bahamas, Nassau," she said. "As I was saying, I was told I needed more training, so I took up secretarial science at Dekalb Community College. When I finished, I still couldn't find a job. My problem was I didn't have any experience working in America." She laughed. "My dear, it seems that I can't win for losing," she said, spreading her hands in a helpless gesture.

I nodded.

"So, when I saw you and the other lady...."

"My mama," I said.

Her eyebrows rose. "Well, my dear, when I saw two black ladies representing a distinguished lawyer like Sidney Jacoby, I said to myself, Meredith, these women might be able to help you get out of this domestic-service trap."

The waitress brought our lunch.

Meredith picked up her fork, stuck a piece of fish with it, put it into her mouth, chewed, and swallowed. "You're going to help me?" she asked.

"Do you want to work in a bank?" I asked.

"My dear," she said, "all I want to do is work in some kind of office. I can't stand housework any longer."

I sat contemplating what she was asking, staring across at her, trying to assess her possibilities. Nothing came to mind, so I said, "I'll see if I can get some kind of leads for you, but I can't promise anything."

Meredith gave me a dimpled smile. "My dear," she said, "I'll be grateful for whatever you find it in your heart to do."

For the remainder of the meal, we talked about Atlanta, my work, and several social functions that I suggested she attend. While we talked, I began to like her and I began to feel she liked me. I told her about my recent trip to Nassau. "I couldn't get a bargain at the straw market," I said. "I had been told by my hostesses never to pay the asking price, but I couldn't get what I wanted any cheaper."

"There is an art to bargaining with my people, my dear," she said.

"It's an art I've yet to learn," I confessed.

An hour later, I paid for the lunch and said good-bye to Meredith, assuring her that I would try to scout out a few leads for her that might lead her to another kind of employment.

The rest of the afternoon I spent on the sixth floor in our law library, struggling with the vacillating thoughts about my father.

Chapter Sixteen

Four days later, at 6:00 A.M., I was awakened by the simultaneous ringing of the telephone and the alarm clock. I rolled over, pushed the alarm, and picked up the phone. It was Mama.

"Simone," she said, her voice tired enough to make me concerned, "I don't want to upset you, but something has happened."

I sat up in bed. "What's wrong?" I asked. "Has somebody else turned up dead?"

"No," she said, her voice dropping, "James is missing!"

"Wait a minute," I said. "What do you mean he's *missing*?"

She took a deep breath. "The last time I saw him," she said, "was the morning after our discussion in the kitchen. He went to work on Monday morning and hasn't been home all week."

I was sick. "Why did you wait so long to call me?" I asked.

"Because I was trying to find him myself," she said. "I called all of his friends, and together we checked out every conceivable place where James could be, but we couldn't find him. I've been sitting here all night hoping he would call. After he didn't, all I could think of to do was to call you."

My feet hit the floor. "I'll be home in a few hours!" I said.

"I'll be expecting you," she said, her voice waning.

I hesitated. "Mama," I began, "if Cliff can get away, I'd like to bring him with me."

"It's all right," she said without any resistance.

By mid-afternoon, Cliff and I were sitting at Mama's table. Today, the smell in her kitchen was that of coffee; Mama hadn't cooked in four days.

"Has Daddy ever done this before?" I asked, trying to figure out what could have happened.

Mama was silent for a moment but shook her head. "No," she said, her voice exasperated, "although he has stayed out all night, you know, when he's had a little too much to drink."

Cliff nodded his head.

"But," Mama continued, "James has never stayed away this long without letting me know how to get in touch with him. He's always been concerned that, if something happened to me, he would want to know right away!"

"You think something bad has happened to him?" I asked.

"I don't know," she said. "It's just not like James, the way he's been acting."

"Something *is* wrong," Cliff said, "and when we find him we're going to make him tell us what it is."

Mama nodded. "I should have pressed James before now," she said. "I knew he was holding something back, but I was hoping and praying that he would trust me enough to confide in me without my pushing."

"He doesn't trust anybody," I said.

"Don't say that about your father, Simone," Mama said.

I frowned.

"James is mixed up with these murders in some way, and he's scared about his involvement. Once we solve the murders, things will be good again, you'll see!"

"If he didn't kill Danny and Janie, how could he be involved?" I asked.

"I don't know," Mama said, "but I've got an idea."

"What do you think?" Cliff asked.

"It's about the gun," Mama said, "but I can't say for sure until I confirm my suspicion with James."

There was a knock at the door.

"Here we go again," I said.

Startled, Mama raised an eyebrow.

"I'll get it," I said, walking out of the kitchen to the front door.

I looked through the peephole and saw a beautiful

white Mercedes sitting in the driveway. At the front door stood four men, buddies of my father. I opened the door.

The first man who walked in was named Buck. He had smooth black skin that was highlighted by a head full of snow-white hair.

The next man was Callahan. His skin was lighter, banana colored, with small brown freckles. His hair was reddish brown. His nickname was "Red."

Denver followed Red. He was tall, thin, and the most garrulous of the bunch. He had a grin on his face, although his eyes were always puffy and blood-shot red.

The last to come in was Coal. He looked to be about forty and he spoke in a clear, articulate voice. He was of medium height and had broad shoulders and beautiful dark brown eyes. His expression was stoic, perhaps indifferent.

It was Coal who spoke. "We came to see your mama," he said, looking past me toward the kitchen. "We've heard from James and we've got a message."

"Come in," I said, motioning them to continue toward the back of the house. The four men walked into the kitchen and nodded a greeting. I introduced them to Cliff. "Mama," I said, "they've heard from Daddy."

Mama looked suspicious. "James called you before he called me?" she said.

"I'm sorry, Candi," Coal said. "We knew where James was all the time, but we didn't want to tell you until...."

Mama butted in, keeping her eyes on Coal. "You knew that I was worried sick about James and you kept his whereabouts a secret?"

"We wanted James to know...."

Mama gazed at Coal. "Know what?" she asked, her voice a bit colder than I would have expected.

Coal cleared his throat. "Let me begin with what happened to James," he said, his voice emotionless. "You'll understand better why we didn't tell you."

Mama was guarded. She took a deep breath and nodded. I glanced toward Cliff, who smiled.

"Last Monday morning," Coal began, "James came over to Red's house."

Red nodded.

"He was upset, so Red gave him a couple of beers to calm him down, you know...."

"Yeah," Red said, "my man's hands were shaking like a leaf from a tree."

"Anyway," Coal started again, "Red gave him a few beers and...."

Mama's eyes narrowed. "In the morning?" she asked. "What has happened to my husband?"

Coal looked past Mama toward the window. "James broke down and said that he was kinda scared that he might be charged with murdering those two kids in the woods because...."

"Because what?" I said, my voice so loud that Cliff frowned at me and shook his head to warn me off.

"Because it was his gun that killed the children," Coal blurted out.

151

I looked at Mama. She seemed relieved by the revelation. "I thought so," she said, as if talking to herself.

I felt as if I had been hit over the head with a ton of bricks. "That doesn't make sense," I said. "If Daddy's gun killed Danny and Janie, it means that he is the prime suspect!"

Red hesitated, then spoke. "That's the problem," Red said. "Your daddy doesn't know whether he used the gun or not."

Mama's eyes widened. "Red," she said, her tone a little less sharp, "what are you talking about?"

"James wants to tell you about it," Red said.

Denver cut in. "We talked it over with him this morning, and he wants you to know what's been bothering him," he said. "But he wants to tell you himself."

"For god sake," Mama said, "where is he?"

For a full minute nobody spoke. Finally Coal said, "He's in the VA hospital in Charleston. In detox!"

A heavy silence fell over the room. Questions twisted like serpents in my mind. All I could think of was that I wanted to see my father, to touch him, to talk to him.

"James in detox," Mama said, her voice surprised. "I knew that he had been drinking a lot more, knew he was coming home later...."

I heard myself speak, but it didn't sound like me talking. "I'm surprised you didn't say something to him about his drinking," I said, looking toward my mother.

She stood, shaking her head, but she didn't reply.

Denver cleared his throat. "He's been drinking pretty heavily for the past few months," he said. "He's tried to hide it from you, Candi; that's why he's been coming home so late."

Red spoke. "We tried to get him to cut down, but he wouldn't listen."

"You should have told me," Mama said, finding her voice at last. "If you're his friends, you would have told me and I would have...."

Buck spoke, his eyes shifting toward Red. "You know how easy it is to get drinks in the military," he said. "It's something we all had to wrestle with, but James always seemed to be able to handle it."

Callahan spread his hands. "It's just since this thing with Danny that it has started getting out of hand for James. Something about his relationship with the boy that seemed to take James over the edge. Anyway, he just couldn't get a grip on it, so...."

"So," Coal interrupted, "when James got to Red's house, he had already had his limit."

"I didn't know that at the time," Red said. "I'd never have given my buddy another drink if...."

"Well," Coal continued, "Red did give him another drink, and he broke down and cried. Red couldn't handle it, so he called the three of us, James' buddies, and we went over to Red's house to see about helping him."

"He was in no shape to talk to you, Candi," Red said again.

Mama stared into the men's faces. Her eyes flared. "No matter what shape James was in," she said, "he is my husband and you should have called me before you decided to do anything for him or with him!"

"We're sorry," Denver said. "We talked it over and decided that the most important thing for us to do at the time was to get help for James."

"He would have done it for us," Buck said.

"He did for me more times than I'd like to say," Red whispered, hanging his head.

Mama shook her head but said nothing.

"Anyway," Denver continued, leaning away from Mama's reach. "We decided to get James back into control of himself and then let him decide what he wanted to do."

"That happened this morning," Coal said, his eyes riveted on Mama's face.

Red spoke. "He's come out of it, and he's asking for you, Candi," he said. "The first thing he said when we visited him this morning was that we should come and tell you."

Mama smiled a small but distinct smile. "He's all right then," she whispered, satisfied that Daddy's absence was not voluntary.

"He's fine," Coal said, noting the softness in Mama's voice. "but he wants to tell you about his gun."

"He wants to tell you himself what he knows about those two murders," Red said.

A lump formed in my throat. "What do you mean?" I asked.

All three sighed. Coal spoke, his words clear, "Your father's drinking has affected him more than he would like."

"How?" I asked.

"The reason he has been so evasive about the last time he met with Danny is that he can't remember very much about what happened!"

I walked over and threw my arms around my mother; for the second time since this ordeal had begun, I felt her body shiver.

Chapter Seventeen

Cliff drove; I sat in front and Mama sat in the backseat of the Honda. The atmosphere was so thick you could cut it with a knife. Daddy's buddies had left the house a half hour earlier and we were speeding toward Waterboro, where we would take 68 into Charleston.

Cliff switched on the radio, and I reached over and turned the sound down so low it was barely audible. He started to turn it up, but I raised my eyebrow and he decided against it. As we drove, Cliff flipped stations a couple of times, then turned the radio off. Mama didn't say a word until we pulled up in front of the hospital parking lot.

"I appreciate you coming," she said, looking at Cliff, "but I want to make sure it's okay with

James...." Her voice trailed off.

Cliff nodded.

"Go park the car," I said to Cliff. "If it's okay with Daddy, I'll come get you from the lobby."

"Okay," he said.

Mama smiled. "Thanks," she said. "It's just that I don't know how James is feeling."

Cliff touched Mama's hand. "I understand," he said. "If it's okay with him, it's okay with me. Whatever he wants he'll get."

Mama and I entered the hospital lobby, which was no more than a large room with chairs lined in rows. In front of the elevators was a reception desk, where we obtained Daddy's room number.

The elevator took us up to the eighth floor. A group of nurses were whispering together behind a big counter right across from the elevators, and they glanced up when we appeared but said nothing to us. As we walked down the hall, we passed several open doorways. It was at the end of the corridor on the left-hand side that we found room 802.

We walked into a room that was large, a long rectangle with several beds in it, hidden behind white curtains. I couldn't tell if they were occupied. The floor was light blue, the tiles darker in some spots. There were three small windows formed by a slit in the side of the building. They looked out onto the hospital parking lot.

A television set hung on brackets hooked into the ceiling over the beds.

As we looked around the room, we heard Daddy

clear his throat and call out, "Candi, over here." He was sitting on the edge of a bed at the far end of the room.

"James," Mama said, her voice gentle. When she reached him, she leaned over and kissed him on the mouth.

"Candi," he said, "I'm sorry." He had on a white hospital gown, a pair of pants, shoes, and socks. He had shaved.

Mama looked at him and gave her hand a little wave to dismiss the apology. "I tried to clean up," he said. "The fellows brought me what they thought I could use."

"They're good friends," Mama said.

He nodded. "Don't be too hard on them," he said. "They did what they thought was right."

"I know," Mama said. "And I'm glad you've lived such a life that you've got friends who care enough about you to do what is best for you."

Daddy looked at me, and I felt myself shift my weight from one foot to the other. "I'm sorry, baby," he whispered. "This ain't right for you and I know it."

"What happened?" I heard myself asking.

"I don't know," he said. "Things just got out of hand, and the next thing I knew I was here." He waved his hands to sweep the room.

For several moments nobody said a word, as if nobody wanted to talk. Then I walked over to my father and put my arms around him. "I'm glad you're all right," I whispered.

"It'll be good again," he said, "like it used to be, I promise...."

I cut him off. "I know," I said, stepping away so that I wouldn't obstruct Mama's eye contact.

"James," Mama said, "Cliff is here, down in the lobby."

I waited, guarded.

"He's been with us all through this thing, and...."

Daddy interrupted. "So?"

"Is it all right for him to come up to the room?"

"Is he special to you, baby?" he asked.

"Yes," I said.

"Special enough to know our business?" he asked.

"Yes," I said. "He knows all."

Daddy grunted. "This ain't the best way to see your going-to-be father-in-law, is it?"

"This is only one time," Mama said. "It'll never happened again."

"I guess I don't see anything wrong with discussing things in front him. If you want him, baby," he said, looking at me, "he can come up."

I reached over and kissed Daddy's cheek again. "Thanks," I said. "It's been good to have Cliff with me through all of this." I left the room, satisfied that it was right to allow my parents to be alone for a while. When I found Cliff in the lobby, I told him that Daddy said it was okay for him to come up but that I wanted to give Mama some time alone with him. We decided to find a coffee shop nearby and have a cup of coffee.

An hour later, Cliff and I got off the elevator and entered my father's room. He and Mama were sitting on the edge of the bed, and he was shaking his head. "I don't know," he was saying, "I guess I didn't want to admit that I needed...." His voice trailed off.

Cliff and I watched each other in silence until Daddy looked up and saw us. "How you doing?" he said, looking at Cliff.

"Pretty good," Cliff said.

"I've done better," Daddy said.

Cliff and I stood holding hands.

Mama leaned closer to Daddy. "When did things start to go downhill?" she asked.

Daddy smiled. "I don't know," he said. "I guess when I started taking time with the boy."

"I was surprised you spent so much time with him," she said.

"Yeah, well you know how clumsy and awkward he was and I, well, I thought I could help him build his confidence, you know, help him go into manhood."

Mama nodded. "You're good at that," she said.

Daddy coughed. "I don't know," he said. "The more time I spent with the boy the more I enjoyed being with him, but at the same time...." He hesitated.

"What?" I asked.

Daddy looked at me. "I'm sorry, Simone," he said. "This never should have happened."

"It's okay, Daddy," I said. "It's okay."

"This is not the way our family life is," he said, addressing Cliff.

"I know, sir," Cliff said. "This is just one of those

things that happens sometimes."

"It won't happen again." Daddy turned to look at Mama. "Candi, I promise this will never happen again."

"I know," she said. Mama waited for a minute. "Tell us more about Danny," she said in a coaxing voice.

Daddy yawned. "It's the medication," he said. "But I'm not going to sleep."

Mama leaned forward and wiped at Daddy's cheek with her hand. "I won't let you go to sleep," she said.

"Well, Candi," Daddy returned to Mama's question about Danny, "I guess while I enjoyed being with the boy it also reminded me of how much I missed our boys."

Mama smiled.

Daddy searched Mama's face. "You know I always saw it in your eyes, how much you missed them."

"They're happy," she said with a look meant to comfort him, "and they're doing what they want to do."

Daddy continued. "Yes, but I know it's my fault that they don't come home more often. And," he hesitated, "I know you blame me."

"No, I don't," Mama protested, trying to ease Daddy's conscience.

Daddy waved his hands toward her. "Now, Candi, don't deny it," he said, his voice becoming stronger. "It's my fault that they're so dedicated to their careers that they can't seem to find time to come see us, or even call."

Mama sighed as if it was hopeless to try to convince him otherwise.

"Anyway," he said, his voice indicating that he was becoming his old self again, "when I started taking up time with the boy, I began remembering all the years I didn't spend with my own boys and I guess it made me sick. So, while I was enjoying helping Danny, I was also yearning for the years I'd missed with my own boys!"

I swallowed; Cliff squeezed my hand.

"And Danny was rather pitiful," Daddy continued. "He had been raised by a smothering mother, had no father or man in his life, and he needed a man to talk to. For some reason, he picked me."

"He picked a good man," Mama said.

For the first time Daddy smiled, and I knew that he was satisfied that Mama would understand what had happened to him and would stand by him.

"I have to admit," he said, "I gave the boy money, let him wear my jacket, my watch, you know."

"Why?" I asked.

"Because it made him feel good," he said. "Made him feel like he had somebody special to take care of him."

"And," Mama said, "it made you feel good to have somebody to take care of."

"The boys are gone, and soon Simone will be too," he said, his voice a bit sulky.

"Come on," I teased. "You ain't about to get rid of me," I said.

Cliff smiled. "Even if you do give her to me," he said, "she'll always be your little girl. That'll never change."

Daddy grinned. "You're right about that, son," he said. "As long as you got that idea, you can have my daughter."

We laughed.

"Tell me more about Danny," Mama prodded.

Daddy shrugged. "Okay," he said, shifting his body to sit back farther on the bed and pulling Mama after him. "Like I said, the boy needed me and I tried to help him. I even promised him that, after he started working, I would help him get his own car, and he liked that idea."

"I guess so," I murmured.

"You knew about the girl, didn't you?" Mama asked.

Daddy shook his head. "No," he said. "I tell you what happened. A couple of months ago, Danny confided in me that he was having a problem."

"A problem?" Cliff asked.

"Yeah, you know. His body wanted a girlfriend but he didn't know how to go about getting one."

Cliff nodded. "Oh, that kind of problem," he said.

"Yes," Daddy said.

"What did you tell him?" Mama asked, her tone non-judgmental.

"I told him what I know," Daddy said.

"And that was?" she asked.

"I told him to go to a town like Savannah, go to a juke joint, and meet an experienced woman who would help him cross over into manhood," he said.

"So that's how he met Janie Pope," I said, staring at him. "You told that poor boy to go buy himself a whore, did you?"

"N-No," Daddy stammered, "I didn't tell him that. I told him to get an experienced woman, that's all."

I was livid. "It's the same thing," I scolded. Cliff cleared his throat and tightened the grip on my hand.

"No, it's not," Daddy grumbled. "And don't try to make me believe I told the boy anything wrong. I told him to find him a girl who wasn't much older than he was but make sure she'd had more experience in life."

I looked at Cliff out of the corner of my eye. He was shaking his head to tell me I shouldn't press my father any further. But I ignored him. "You corrupted a young boy," I said, my voice softer.

"I did no such thing, did I, Candi?" Daddy insisted.

"That wasn't the kind of advice you gave our boys, was it?" Mama asked, her words soft-spoken.

Daddy lowered his head but didn't answer.

I was angry, but Mama bridged the moment by saying, "I don't agree with you, James, but that's water under the bridge, and there's nothing that can be done about it now."

Daddy nodded.

Mama continued. "You did give Danny money to take this young lady out on a date, didn't you?"

Daddy nodded. "A couple of times," he whispered.

"According to Janie's mother, you gave Danny enough money to visit Janie more than a couple of times."

"It was no harm," Daddy said. "The girl knew what to expect, and I made sure that Danny had enough to keep her happy."

164

Mama took a deep breath, then let it out. "So, what happened the last night you saw Danny?" she asked.

"That's what I've got to tell you," he said, his eyes pleading, "I don't know what happened, Candi. I swear, I can't remember much about it!"

Chapter Eighteen

Mama reached over and touched Daddy's hand. There was not even a slight sign of irritation in her manner. In fact, there was an almost peaceful look on her face that seemed to make Daddy's handsome features more pronounced. Still, there was the puzzlement and pent-up tears in his eyes. The moment of quietness grew into minutes.

A doctor appeared. It was as if he had sneaked up on us. I didn't hear him approach; he materialized next to Daddy's bed. He was tall and thin, with short gray hair, and he was wearing a white lab coat.

"I'm Dr. Reed," he said, extending his hand. He gave Cliff a handshake, then me, then Mama. His handshake was firm. He stepped to the foot of Daddy's bed. When he spoke, his manner was cordial, as if he had known all of us for quite a long time.

"James is a very strong guy," he said, first looking at Daddy and then at each of us. I felt a surge of heat rush up my neck and into my face. I didn't look at my father.

"He's had a bad time of it, but it's all over now, isn't it, James?"

"I know what I have to do now, doc," he said.

"You don't have to worry about him," the doctor assured Mama. "I'm sure this was a temporary situation, something that's quite common in this environment." He waved his hands around the room.

We smiled but said nothing.

After a thoughtful silence, Daddy asked, "When can I go home?"

I felt myself holding my breath and tightening the grip on Cliff's hand.

The doctor laughed, as if he understood the pleading look in Daddy's eyes. "When do you want to go?" he asked.

"Today," he said, his voice rising. "Now, with my family."

"Get your things together," Dr. Reed said, smiling. "I'll see that the papers are put through by the time you get down to the lobby."

"Thanks, doc," Daddy said as Mama squeezed his hand. I let out my breath and nodded.

"Thanks," we all said in unison.

"It was a temporary thing," he said, waving his hand toward Daddy. "But, if you need to come back, James, you won't hesitate, will you?"

Daddy shook his head. "I won't be coming back, doc," he said confidently.

"But, if you do need to...."

Daddy interrupted. "I'll come back," he said.

Mama smiled. "I'll see to it," she said.

The doctor was satisfied. He winked and made a circle with his thumb and index finger, then said good-bye and walked out of the room.

Daddy looked at Mama and said, "This won't happen again, Candi, I promise."

"I know," she said. "Now, let's get out of here."

Grinning, Daddy pulled his things from underneath the nightstand next to his bed.

Forty-five minutes later there was a wonderful sense of release as we climbed into the car and headed toward Hampton.

When we got home, Mama filled the kitchen with the delicious smell of fresh-brewed coffee while she microwaved something she had taken out of the freezer for us to eat. Daddy sat at the kitchen table, watching Mama work her magic with food.

"Candi," he said, sipping from his cup, "I am so hungry for your cooking...."

"I haven't been able to cook a thing in the past four days," she said.

"Well, you've had your vacation," he teased. "Now, back to feeding your old man."

We laughed.

In less than an hour Mama had spread the table with baked chicken, walnut dressing, pickled beets, field peas and okra, brown-and-serve rolls, and honey butter. "This is the best I can do," she said.

The meal was over, the dishes were in the dishwasher, and we were having a piece of coconut cake and a second cup of coffee when Mama brought up the subject of Danny again.

"James," she said, her voice sweet, "tell me what you do remember about the last time you saw Danny."

Daddy put his fork down on his plate, took a deep breath, and leaned back in his seat. "I guess now is as good a time as any," he said. "I know you want to talk about that boy again."

"We have to find out who killed those children," Mama said, "since you think they were killed with your gun."

"I know," he said, almost to himself.

"You know too that, as soon as Abe finds the gun and runs a check on it, it will be traced to you."

Daddy nodded.

"And, since you don't remember much about what happened during the past few months, a pretty good circumstantial case can be made against you," I said.

Daddy raised his eyebrows. "Yes," he said, sighing again. "What do you want to know, Candi?"

Mama looked serious. "Everything," she said. "Everything about you and the boy."

Daddy cleared his throat. "Well," he began, "as I told you at the hospital, the boy took a liking to me."

"Yes," I said, "and you...."

Cliff interrupted. "Simone," he said, waving his hand. "Let your father tell his story without interruptions, please!"

I wanted to protest but I decided against it. "Okay," I said.

Daddy smiled and touched Cliff's hand. "You're all right," he said.

Cliff nodded.

"Well," Daddy started again, forcing himself to keep his tone upbeat. "Candi, you know the boy would wait for me to come home so he could talk to me. Well, as I told you before, a couple of times we arranged to meet in the woods behind his house."

Mama looked puzzled. "I thought his waiting for you in the yard was often enough," she said.

Daddy shrugged his shoulders. "There were times I worked late," he said. "You know, a couple of times during the month I have to work overtime."

"Go on," Mama nudged.

"Well, I had given the boy my work number."

"So he could call you when he needed you," I said. Cliff rolled his eyes.

"Yes," Daddy said, an edge in his voice, "and he called me on June fifth."

"Simone, please!" Mama said. I shifted in my chair. After a moment, Mama spoke again. "And you met him," she said.

For a moment he hesitated, then spoke. "Not before I...." His voice trailed off.

"You had a few beers," Mama said, as if she knew that Daddy would not be comfortable admitting he had a drinking problem.

"Yes," he said. "It turned out that I didn't have to work overtime that day after all, so I went with the fellows to a local bar and had a few beers until it was time for me to meet the boy."

"Do you remember whether or not Danny was waiting when you got there?" Mama asked.

"N-No," Daddy stammered. "I think I had to wait for him, but I don't know how long I waited."

Mama looked as if something was clicking in her mind. "When he got there, what do you remember about him?"

Daddy sat up straighter. "I don't know," he said. "I guess he looked the same. I can't remember anything special."

"Did he have on shoes?"

Daddy raised one eyebrow. "You keep asking that question," he said. "In those woods in the beginning of summer, the cockleburs would have torn his feet up if he didn't have on any shoes!"

"That's true," Mama said. "What did he say to you?" she asked.

"I don't know," Daddy said. "I guess he wanted money; that's the only reason he ever called me."

"So you gave him money?"

"I guess so."

"Did he say he wanted money to give to the girl?" she asked.

Daddy thought for a minute. "I don't remember, Candi," he said. He hesitated, then said, "Seems like he said something about a telephone bill; I don't know."

"What about the gun?" I asked, no longer able to sit. Cliff frowned, but I ignored him.

"I didn't miss the gun until after the boy's body was found," Daddy said.

"What made you think the gun that killed those kids was yours?" Mama asked.

"Something, sometime or other, I can't remember when, but I had the gun in the pocket of the car to take it to the base to have it cleaned. Danny saw it and took it out. I made him put it back."

"You didn't loan Danny the gun?" she asked.

"No, Candi," he said. "And I swear the boy didn't take it out of my car."

"What made you think he wouldn't steal?" I snapped.

Cliff turned toward me. He looked straight into my eyes without blinking. "Simone," he said, "just keep quiet and listen!"

I began pouting, leaning back in my chair and folding my arms.

"He's never taken anything before," Daddy said, his voice a little shaky. "Anything he asked for I gave to him. He had no reason to steal from me."

Tempted to argue that statement, I opened my mouth, then shut it when I saw Cliff's stare. I looked at my watch; it was ten o'clock. I yawned but nobody seemed interested in the time, so I slouched down in my chair.

Mama smiled, then began speaking again. "Back to June fifth, the last night you saw Danny," she said. "What happened next?"

"I don't remember," he said, clenching and unclenching his fists. "When I got home, you were out. It was one of those nights you go to your club meeting, so I went to bed. I didn't think about the boy, the gun, or anything else until I hadn't seen or heard from him for about a week."

There was a slight frown on Mama's face. "And Lucy's proclamation that something had happened to him," she said.

The lines in Daddy's face deepened. "Yeah, that too," he said. "When you told me that Lucy swore that something had happened to the boy and I realized that I hadn't seen or heard from him, I got worried."

"What made you think that you were responsible for his death?" Cliff asked.

"I don't know," Daddy said. "The whole night was a big cloud in my mind, so confusing. I liked the boy and I didn't like him. I don't understand it myself. Danny needed me, but he was getting on my nerves…, always waiting or calling me…, asking for things…, talking about things that I didn't know much about. I hated what was happening but I didn't know how to stop it. You know, Candi, he always made me feel so guilty."

Mama walked over and put her arms around Daddy's neck. "You could never have hurt those children," she said.

"I was miserable, Candi," he said. "The boy had his hands flat on my heart, like a knife; he was ripping it out of my chest. I felt like a slave, trying to help him, trying to forget that I hadn't helped my own boys. I have to be honest and say that, whenever I'd

have a little too much to drink, I thought about...."
His voice trailed off.

"Even when you've had a lot to drink," Mama said, "and you feel your guts being torn apart, you couldn't be a murderer, James. That's why you were drinking, trying to kill the pain of losing your own boys."

"I'm sorry, Candi," Daddy said.

Mama shook her head.

"No," Daddy continued, looking up into Mama's eyes. "Let me say it, please."

"Okay," Mama nodded.

He was silent for a moment, thinking things over. "I'm sorry because I wouldn't give my boys the time, the patience, the love."

"I know," Mama said.

Daddy sounded bewildered. "I'm sorry that I gave you two sons and then made you sacrifice them."

Mama stood, rubbing Daddy's shoulders. She thought for a while, then, with a sparkle in her eyes, she spoke, changing the subject. "James," she said, "I think I know who killed those children." She had that look that told me she was on to the solution to this mess. "I'm going to set a trap for the killer. "And Simone...," Mama added, turning to me.

I looked up, puzzled.

"You and Cliff are going to help me!" she said.

Chapter Nineteen

The next morning, Mama cooked breakfast: linked sausages, scrambled eggs, candied spiced apples, grits, and buttermilk biscuits. She squeezed fresh orange juice. There wasn't much conversation during the meal; nobody wanted to pause long enough to talk.

After breakfast, Daddy went to the bedroom to lie down. The medication that Dr. Reed had given him made him sleepy. He was still on leave from his job, and, earlier that week, Mama had arranged to get time off from work as well. After the dishes were washed, she, Cliff, and I sat down to work to comb through pages of telephone bills.

"What are we looking for again?" I asked.

"James said the last time he saw Danny was the night of June fifth. I want to see if a telephone call was made to Janie's house on or around that date."

"Bingo," Cliff said.

"Where?" Mama asked.

Cliff circled the date of the call. It was June fifth, the place called was Savannah, Georgia, the time 9:30 A.M. The length of the call had been fifteen minutes. "That's the last call made to that number," he said.

"Then that's it," Mama said, grinning. "There wouldn't have to be another call after Danny's death, would there?" she said. "That would have given Janie plenty of time to get to Camp Branch. Now, Simone, you and I are going to have a nice little visit with Rose Smart, Esther's closest neighbor and friend."

"Rose's house again?" I asked.

"Yes," she said. "We need to talk to her, but first we need to go to the sheriff's office to set our trap!"

The sun had set and the sky was a deep navy blue, edging closer to black. Stars were coming out one by one. There was no moon. The night was quiet; there was the sound of crickets chirping in the woods. I stared out of the window as we drove toward Camp Branch.

"Thank goodness this mess is almost over," I said, turning to look at Mama. "It's been hard on all of us."

"It's been hardest on James," she said.

I was annoyed by her calmness. "If he had said something before now...."

Mama cut in. "James is proud," she said. "He doesn't like to think he needs anybody."

"I know," I said, feeling a little guilty. "You know I love him, don't you, Mama?"

"Yes," she said.

"I don't mean to be so hard on him; it's just that, if he had told us...."

"He will talk more in the future," she said. "He promised me that he would."

"I'm glad to know he didn't love Danny more than he loved his own sons."

"I always knew that," she said.

"Be honest," I said. "You thought Danny was his son, didn't you?"

Mama shook her head. "I told you James is not a liar, and he denied being the boy's father and I believed him."

"Well, I wasn't so sure," I said. "Offering five thousand dollars to find the boy was a bit much for me to accept on blind faith."

Mama smiled, acknowledging that she understood how I felt. We crossed the railroad track. "He told me he thought that, if Danny was hiding out someplace, say in Savannah, and knew that he was going to pay so much money for his whereabouts, he would show up."

"The boy was a con artist," I said. "He would have showed up and found a reason to talk Daddy into giving him the money."

"I don't think he was as bad as that, Simone," she said.

"Mama, please don't be naive. Danny used Daddy, and you know it."

"Simone, the boy never had anybody to take an interest in him, nobody to make him feel special."

"Yeah, sure," I said.

"Remember when you were a little girl," Mama said, "and your daddy would come home from overseas?"

"How can I forget?" I said.

"Remember all the presents he used to bring you and your brothers?"

"I've got dolls from Japan that I keep in my room to this day."

"How did those presents make you feel?" Mama asked.

"Special, I guess."

"Now, imagine if you never had anybody to make you feel that way."

"He had his mother."

"He didn't need that kind of mother love," Mama said. For a moment, neither of us spoke. "Well," I said as we were turning off onto the dirt road that led to Rose's driveway, "this mess will be over soon and things will be good again, like they used to be!"

As we were climbing out of the car, Rose's doorway filled with light. "Who is out there?" Rose yelled.

"It's us, Rose," Mama answered. "Candi and Simone Covington."

Fifteen minutes later we were sitting in Rose's living room, drinking diet soft drinks.

"Well I'm glad you stopped by," Rose was saying, "I took Esther to Columbia the other day to see Lucy."

"How is Lucy?" Mama asked.

"Pitiful," she said, frowning. "I talked to the doctor and he doesn't think she'll ever be able to come home again."

"Did Lucy mention Danny?" I asked.

"Yeah, kept saying something had happened to the boy out in the woods. Neither Esther nor I had the heart to tell her that the boy was dead."

"She didn't come home for the funeral?" Mama asked.

"No way," Rose said. "She's pretty bad off."

"Well," Mama said, "I guess we'll have to visit her again soon."

I frowned, hoping Rose wouldn't see the expression on my face.

"That'll be good," she said, either not seeing my expression or ignoring it.

"Heard anything about who the girl is that they found in the woods?" Rose asked.

"No," Mama said, touching her head with her hand. "But, I did hear that Sheriff Abe is going to stop looking for whoever killed the girl and Danny."

Rose gave Mama a cold stare. "No," she said, her voice dramatic.

"Yeah," Mama said, glancing toward me. Her eyes seemed to twinkle. "He told me that he's just about decided the killer was somebody just wandering through the woods, you know, a stranger."

Rose stared at us, her mouth open.

"It's a shame," Mama said, sounding appalled. "Abe said it will end up in the dead file, you know, as one of those cases that goes unsolved."

"That is a shame," Rose repeated Mama's words. "And poor Esther was so sure that Abe would find out who killed her boy. I don't know if she can take having it end this way."

"Whoever killed the boy killed the girl," I whispered. "And the rest of the girl's body parts have not been found." I shook my head.

"That girl ain't from around here," Rose said. "Nobody's missing a child. Somebody killed her away from here and dropped the body."

"I don't know," I said. "Looks like the sheriff will have two unsolved killings on his hands."

Rose shook her head in disbelief. "Are you sure there ain't no clue, no way of them finding out who killed Danny?" she asked.

Mama shook her head. "Abe said he hasn't found anything to even point to a suspect."

Rose leaned in her chair. She looked as if she didn't believe Mama. "I declare," she said.

I shrugged. "It would be good if they could find the gun," I said, loud enough to be heard but low enough to give the impression that I was thinking out loud.

"What?" Rose asked, interested.

"The gun," I said, forcing myself to look into Rose's eyes. "The one that killed both Danny and the girl."

Rose squirmed in her chair. I could see wheels turning inside her head. "How will that help the sheriff?" she asked.

Mama spoke, keeping her voice low and quiet. "If they find the gun, they can run a tracer on it and learn who owned it. Once they know the owner, Abe can make him confess to the killing."

For a moment Rose sat with a deep frown in her brow. She looked into Mama's eyes. "Did he search the woods for the gun?" she asked.

Mama shook her head. "Abe said he and his deputies went through those woods with a fine tooth comb, but nothing turned up, not a clue to who killed the children."

Rose stiffened just for a moment, then stopped herself. "I declare," she said, her voice calm.

Mama sucked her teeth and shook her head. "My heart goes out to poor Esther," she said.

Rose flinched, as if she was surprised by Mama's sympathy. "I bet it does," she said.

Mama ignored the cutting tone. "The poor woman's sister is in the state hospital, her boy killed, and the person who killed him is walking around scot-free, like he ain't done a thing!"

Rose grunted. "Lord have mercy on us all," she said, jumping up out of her chair. "If that person gets away with killing poor innocent Danny, none of us can sleep easy in our beds!"

The clock on the wall chimed the hour; it was ten o'clock. Mama smiled and stood up. "We'd better go," she said, motioning me to stand up. I hesitated, then stood up and walked toward the front door. "We were on our way from Savannah and, as we drove up to the crossing, I thought about you and told Simone that we ought to stop by to see how you were doing."

"I do appreciate you coming by," Rose said, walking with us to the door.

After we were in the car and I was sure Rose cound not hear me, I started mimicking Mama's voice as she had told Rose we would be visiting Lucy in Columbia. "I won't be going with you," I said.

"I know I said some things that weren't quite true," Mama confessed, "but it's the only way to set our trap."

"Well, I hope she takes the bait," I said. "If she doesn't, I don't know how you're going to prove your theory."

"Simone, the killer is a simple country woman who wants James to go to jail for Danny's murder," Mama said, her voice confident. "The assumption we have to make is that she still has the gun. She has tried to steer Abe toward James by leaving his watch and the button from his jacket near the girl's body. Now, if she believes that the only thing that will lead Abe to James is the gun, she'll want him to get it as soon as possible. She thinks that the reason Abe hasn't pinned the murders on James before now is because I haven't given him James' watch or the button from his jacket."

"She's right," I said.

"Be that as it may," Mama continued, "she'll want Abe to get the gun without my interference."

"That makes sense," I said, "I just hope you're right," I said.

"That poor misguided woman," Mama said, shaking her head.

Sunday morning, Cliff and I had just sat down to breakfast with my parents when there was a knock on the door. We looked at each other and smiled.

"The trap has sprung," Mama whispered.

"Thank goodness," I said, getting up to answer the front door. A few minutes later I followed Sheriff Abe

Stanley into the kitchen. "Have a seat," Mama said. "I've already put a plate on the table for you."

Abe took off his hat and grinned. He sat down in the chair next to my father, putting his hat on the back of the kitchen chair. He mocked a blessing, then began tablespooning grits onto his plate. "You were right again, Candi," he said, winking at Mama. "I've got it on that camera you and your boy," he looked at Cliff, who smiled boyishly, "set up at the jail house on Friday."

"He's not our son yet," Daddy said.

"Are you sure you got it all?" Mama asked. "There is no doubt?"

"No doubt at all," the sheriff said, piling his plate with biscuits. "My deputies and I watched the tape before I came over here this morning, and it'll stand up in any court in this state. The picture is as clear as broad daylight."

"Good," Cliff whispered. "I was afraid of messing it up with that bad lighting."

"I tell you it's as clear as broad daylight," Sheriff Abe said, biting onto a piece of bacon. He shook his head in delight, chewing then swallowing. "Candi, you're the best cook in the county."

"Have some more," Mama urged.

"I will," he said. "Soon as I make some room on this here plate, I will."

We laughed.

He ate another mouthful. He looked at Mama again and shook his fork. "I've got the gun, just like you said I would, wrapped up tight and neat."

Daddy cleared his throat but didn't make a comment.

"I told Abe that the gun belongs to you, James," Mama said. "I told him that Danny stole it out of the pocket of your car and you didn't realize it was missing until a few days ago when you were up in Charleston."

Daddy nodded.

Sheriff Abe smiled at Daddy. "Too bad for him," he said. "Maybe if he hadn't taken your gun…, but then who knows what a person will do if they want to do it bad enough, hey Candi?"

Mama nodded.

I waited a minute before I spoke. "I guess the gun doesn't have fingerprints," I said.

The sheriff shrugged his shoulders but he didn't answer; he had a mouthful of grits. "I doubt it," he said after he had swallowed. "But, with this here videotape of Esther putting the gun inside the front door of the jail house, we don't need no fingerprints."

"It's as good as her confession."

Everybody was silent. Then Mama spoke, her voice soft. "What did she leave it in?" she asked.

"Would you believe a shoe box?" Sheriff Abe said. "A sneaker shoe box!"

Chapter Twenty

The dining-room table was set with Mama's hand-made lace tablecloth, her best china, and her crystal stemware. The food was barbecued spare ribs, fried chicken, meat loaf, turnip greens, candied sweet potatoes, baby lima beans, rice, gravy, cole slaw, and fried green tomatoes. On the dessert tray there was peach cobbler, jelly cake, and apple pie.

There were twelve of us: Coal, Red, Denver, Buck, Mama and Daddy, Donna and Ernest, Sheriff Abe, his deputy, and Cliff and I. We were celebrating Mama's victory; she had solved another case. When Sheriff Abe showed Esther the tape of her putting the gun inside the front door of the jail house, she broke down and confessed.

She hadn't intended to kill Danny but didn't have

any choice after he'd found her burying parts of Janie's body. We didn't get a big bonus this time, but we got Daddy's gratitude, and that was more valuable.

"What made you suspect Esther?" Sheriff Abe asked.

"I didn't suspect her at first," Mama said, "but the more I thought about it the more it seemed a plausible explanation."

"Why?" Cliff asked.

"Because there was no logical reason for anybody killing Danny!"

"So?" Cliff asked.

"So, I began to think that Danny might have been killed not because of who he was but because of something that he knew or had seen. That line of reasoning made everything else fall in place!"

"Tell us what happened," Coal said.

Mama smiled. "For one thing," she began, "Esther felt threatened by James giving Danny money and presents. She thought that James wanted to take Danny away from her. And," Mama smiled at Daddy, "some of the money that you had been giving Danny, he had used to pay the telephone bill so that Esther didn't know he was calling Savannah. Anyway, that morning, before Danny called James, Esther found a telephone bill. She raised so much sand that Danny promised to get the money to pay the bill, and that's why he called James.

"Sometime later, when Danny was out of the house, Esther called the number in Savannah and talked to Janie, who admitted that Danny visited her and gave her money. Esther became livid. She told Janie that if she came to Camp Branch she would give her more money than Danny had ever seen. Janie, not thinking much of Danny and being an eager beaver, took the bait and drove to Camp Branch late that afternoon."

A light bulb flashed on in my head. "The car," I said. "The green car I saw out of Esther's kitchen window must have belonged to Janie."

"That's right," Mama said. "Janie drove to Camp Branch, where Esther took her out in the woods and shot her with James' gun. Danny had taken the gun from James' car pocket a few days earlier and Esther had found it along with James' watch and jacket."

"Go on," I said.

"That night, while Danny was meeting James, Esther was out in the woods hacking Janie's body to pieces. I can only speculate about this, but I believe that, when Danny came through the woods from his meeting with James, he thought he heard something, but not seeing anybody he went on to the house."

Daddy shook his head in amazement.

"Danny, as is his habit, took his shoes off on the back porch. After removing them, he no doubt stood looking out into the woods, thinking that somebody was out there."

"Maybe Crazy Joe?" I said.

"Maybe. Anyway he, like Simone, saw Janie's car so, without putting his shoes back on his feet, he ran out to find out what was going on."

"What happened next?" Daddy asked.

"He found his mother burying parts of Janie's body."

"How awful," Donna said.

"Not while we're eating," Red said.

"Anyway," Mama continued, "Danny and his mother began struggling, and Esther got ahold of the gun again and shot him."

"She didn't mean to kill him," Sheriff Abe said.

"No," Mama continued. "Shooting Danny was the last thing Esther wanted to do."

"Since Danny's body was found in the clearing on the other side of the woods, how did it get moved from behind his house?" I asked.

"Esther was in shock after she shot Danny. She moved his body so that it wouldn't be too close to the house..., maybe she didn't want it close to her, I don't know."

"I wonder what made Lucy think that something had happened to Danny," Daddy said.

"Well," Mama said, "this is only my suspicion but, when Lucy said that there was a special look, I think she was talking about a look that she had seen on Esther's face before."

"When?" I asked.

"Maybe when Esther killed the Joneses."

"You don't mean it?" I said.

"Back then, Esther was having an affair with a married man. The old people tried to get her to stop and she killed them. Lucy saw that murderous look on Esther's face at the time that they died. She saw it again when Danny went missing, so she thought that Esther had done something to the boy."

"I guess the murderous look you're talking about

was for Janie Pope," Buck said.

"I'm sure," Mama continued, "but when Lucy started saying that something had happened to Danny, Esther went into the woods and moved Janie's body because she didn't want Janie to be linked to her son."

"Where did she put it?" I asked.

"I don't know, but I'm sure Abe will find the car sooner or later."

The Sheriff nodded.

"In Esther's twisted mind, she blamed James for Danny's death, so she decided that James should go to jail. She didn't make that decision until after Danny's body had been found, so she had to try to tie James to Danny another way."

"How?" Ernest asked.

Mama smiled. "It was Esther who was in the woods the day Simone and I found Janie's body," she explained. "She was the one who put James' watch and the jacket there. She wanted them to be found by Abe so it would look like James had killed the girl. By putting the girl's torso near where Danny's body was found, she figured Abe would link the two deaths and James would be charged with both of them."

"Why did you keep asking about Danny's shoes?" I asked.

"Danny would not take off his shoes except if he was at home or going into his house. Walking without shoes in the woods suggested that he saw or heard something that made him react so quickly he didn't think to put on his shoes. Seeing Janie's car in the back of his house would do that."

"So that's all there is to it?" Donna asked.

"Rose and James both said that Esther kept Danny away from other children. The boy was awkward, couldn't play ball. This suggested that he had been kept sheltered. Also, Trudy Pope had said that it was a woman who called Janie the morning she left home. Remember, she thought it was one of Janie's girlfriends, but in fact it was Esther."

"And the telephone bill?" Ernest asked.

"The money Danny asked me for the last time I saw him?" Daddy said, remembering.

"Yes," Mama smiled. "You said that you thought Danny had said something about paying a telephone bill. I surmised that Danny wanted money to pay the bill that his mother had found with the calls to Janie's house. He didn't know that Esther had called Janie, had lured her to Camp Branch, and had killed her!"

"And our trip to Rose?" I asked.

"Well, if anybody could leave a bug in Esther's ear about the gun, I figured it would be Rose. Esther - didn't trust me. Remember how she pulled away from me when I went to tell her that the sheriff had found Danny's body in the woods? It was clear that she didn't like me."

"Now you know it was because she hated your husband," I said.

Mama nodded.

"How did you know that she would take the gun to Sheriff Abe directly?" Daddy asked.

"I figured Esther would want Abe to get the gun as soon as possible, without my interference. That's why

I made sure to tell Rose that Abe had combed the woods and had found no sign of a gun. I didn't want Esther to think that she could sneak and put it in the woods in the middle of the night, hoping that Abe would still be out there looking for it."

"Why?" Coal asked.

"Because," she laughed, "if she had put it there, we would have had no way of catching her on the video camera."

For several minutes the activity around the table was that of chewing and swallowing. Mama looked at me. "I heard from your brothers, Rodney and Solomon," she said, smiling.

Daddy looked up from his plate.

"What are they up to?" I asked.

"They're planning to visit us the last week in October," she said. "They're both coming and bringing their wives and children..., my grandchildren!"

Daddy smiled but said nothing.

"You'll have to cook," Cliff said.

Mama smiled. "Of course," she said.

"Well," Daddy said, leaning back in his chair and rubbing his stuffed belly, "I know you'll outdo yourself, Candi."

We all laughed. I was glad that things were back to normal!

MAMA SOLVES A MURDER

When Simone's former college roommate is arrested for murder, it appears to be an open-and-shut case, but her boss, Atlanta attorney Sidney Jacoby, takes on the defense and assigns Simone to investigate. This is the kind of case that's right up Mama's alley, so Simone invites her for a visit. Mama's nickname is "Candi" because of her candied sweet potato complexion. She is charming, ingratiating, intuitive, and shrewd; she is also nosy, manipulative, foolhardy, and sometimes absolutely infuriating—but she has a talent for cooking and for solving mysteries.